I0629696

MILK IS FOR GHOSTS

[1]

[SEARCHING DATABASE FOR AUTHOR ID: P_CEPEK]
> 3 RECORDS FOUND:

[2] ─────────────────────────────────────

THE SHAPE OF THE SILENCE (2025)
THEY'RE STILL WRITING ME (2025)
MILK IS FOR GHOSTS (2026)

MILK IS FOR GHOSTS

Stories of Millennial Gothic

[3]

PADRAIC MAHER CEPEK

PADRAIC MAHER CEPEK

[4]

Published by // Ghost Process Press Mundelein, IL

First Edition: January 2026

Library of Congress Control Number: [2026904909] ISBN [**9 7 9 □ 8 □ 2 1 8 □ 9 1 7 5 4 □ 8**]

System Architecture: Cover design by [Name] Interior layout by Padraic Maher Cepek Typeface: Spectral (serif) and Roboto (sans serif).

Printed in the United States of America 979-8-218-91754-8

For those who cannot even be a Lost Generation,
because their forest was deleted.

[5]

PADRAIC MAHER CEPEK

[6]

SYSTEM DIRECTORY

Millennial Gothic

Every generation inherits its own ghosts. In the South, writers once gave us the Southern Gothic—stories of ruined plantations, family secrets, and the weight of history pressing through the floorboards. That form of gothic took root in a landscape scarred by slavery and violence, where the past could never be cleanly buried.

The gothic has never really been about castles or cobwebs. It has always been about dread—the kind that lingers in the structures of everyday life. What makes it endure is its ability to shift, to change shape with the times. If the Southern Gothic belonged to the South's haunted legacy, then what follows is a gothic shaped by the millennial condition.

Millennial Gothic is born from a generation raised on collapse. It trades ruined mansions for supermarkets, classrooms, apps, and endless feeds. Its monsters are not vampires or phantoms but debts that will not die, systems that erase us, and memories we are told to forget. It is a literature where the fluorescent glow of a big-box store feels as uncanny as candlelight in a crypt, and where the algorithms that watch us function like modern-day curses.

This gothic is defined by a few recurring shadows:

- Hauntings that aren't personal but systemic—workers, debts, and histories looping on repeat.
- Inheritance that arrives not as land or legacy but as precarity: student loans, gig work, and climate catastrophe.
- Horror found in paperwork, metrics, queues, and autoplay videos—ordinary rituals that swallow identity whole.
- A struggle between remembering and erasing, between what refuses to be forgotten and what society demands we move past.

[9]

To call it gothic is to recognize that these experiences are not just frustrating or absurd but deeply uncanny.

They carry the weight of something larger than ourselves, something that presses in on the edges of ordinary life until it becomes strange, even terrifying.

Millennial Gothic is the atmosphere of being alive in the early twenty-first century. It is fluorescent and digital, bureaucratic and algorithmic. It tells us that haunting isn't rare—it's ordinary, woven into the systems we move through every day.

Essential Worker

Maya first saw him in March, near the empty apple bins.

An old man in a cardigan, translucent as breath on glass, moving his hands across the display as if polishing invisible fruit. She blinked. Gone. But the smell lingered—antiseptic and something faintly sweet, like rotting pears.

By April, there were more.

The cardigan man. A nurse in faded scrubs by the pharmacy, badge half-slipped through her chest.

A teenager leaning against the cooler doors, his expression fixed somewhere between boredom and shock.

They weren't frightening at first. More like afterimages. But Maya found herself counting them anyway.

She mentioned it to Derek on break.

"You seeing things in there?"

He blew smoke through his mask, squinting. "Like what?"

"People who aren't... all the way here."

Derek's laugh broke into a cough. "We're all not all the way here. I've slept ten hours this week."

He wasn't wrong. Maya's own body felt borrowed, running on fumes and free coffee. Some nights, after closing, she'd sit in her car in the dark lot and picture driving until the tank hit empty. Just driving.

But she never did.

The ghosts grew bolder.

Mrs. Chen appeared on a Thursday, still clutching her reusable bag with the kittens on it. Maya remembered her exact-change ritual—bananas, tea, dumplings, bills folded crisp. Now Mrs. Chen circled the aisles with her bag, but the groceries vanished as she walked.

[11]

Sometimes the ghosts drifted out of their loops.

The teenager crouched near a stack of soda cases, scribbling something onto the floor in condensation. When Maya bent closer, she saw the word repeating, shaky but legible: STAY.

The nurse sat in the pharmacy chair one night, rolling up her sleeve for a flu shot no one gave. Then she looked straight at Maya and raised her other arm, veins mapped in faint blue, lips moving. No sound, but Maya could read the words: your turn.

She tried to tell Derek again.

"I think they know I can see them."

He looked worse than usual—skin gray, cough deeper. "Then don't look."

That night, Maya dreamed of Mrs. Chen at her register, pressing coins into her palm, whispering, count again.

She woke with the smell of tea in her hair.

The company newsletter ran a photo of Maya behind a pyramid of toilet paper, her eyes glazed above the mask. Caption: Our Heroes.

The heroes got a pizza party. Two mediums for forty-three employees. Hazard pay for six weeks.

The ghosts got no mention.

The meeting was in Conference Room B, windowless and humming with the smell of carpet glue. Regional Manager Stevens spoke from a laptop screen propped on expired protein bars.

"Time to get back to normal," he said, his face pixelating. "The worst is behind us."

Through the glass wall, Maya counted seventeen ghosts. Mrs. Chen adjusting her empty bag. The cardigan man rearranging air. The nurse rubbing sanitizer into hands that flickered in and out.

"Customer satisfaction is down," Stevens continued.

"Smiles. Service. You're not just employees—you're the face of our brand."

Maya raised her hand. "What about the people who died?"

Static froze his grin.

Her coworkers stared at the table, shifting. Derek coughed into his sleeve.

When the feed resumed, Stevens said, "Sorry— connection issue. What was that?"

"The customers," Maya repeated, louder. "The ones

who died."

Assistant Manager Rodriguez cut in: "Let's stay positive. Focus on moving forward."

But outside the glass, the teenager pressed his palm against the pane, leaving a wet handprint that didn't fade.

That night, she stocked shelves in silence. Twenty-three ghosts, then twenty-five. Some wandered aisles that no longer existed, walking through walls into phantom departments. One stood in the cereal aisle holding a jar of pickles, eyes locked on her as if waiting for an explanation.

At closing, she found Mrs. Chen again, reading the ingredients on a box of tea. Maya stepped beside her.

"I'm sorry," she whispered.

Mrs. Chen turned, her eyes startlingly clear, her face almost solid. "Don't be," she said. Then she faded, the tea box dropping soundlessly through her arms.

After midnight, Maya clocked out. The lot was empty except for Derek's Honda. She sat in her car, engine off, watching the fluorescent glow of the store through the rain.

Inside, the living kept working. The ghosts kept multiplying.

For a moment she imagined unlocking the doors and letting them in, all of them, until the store overflowed. Letting them sort the apples, ring the registers, stock the shelves.

She imagined herself among them, lighter, her hands moving without weight, free of the beeping scanners and the endless loop of moving forward.

Her key hovered in the ignition.
She didn't turn it.

Mass Shooter Drill

The announcement clicked on at 10:04 a.m.

"This is a drill. Repeat: this is a drill."

Ms. Alvarez rose from her chair and locked the classroom door. She turned off the lights, drew the blinds, and motioned for her students to crouch beneath their desks. The ritual was second nature now: knees to chest, hands still, breaths shallow.

She counted—twenty-four.

When the intercom clicked off, she counted again. Twenty-three.

"Jordan?" she whispered.

His desk was empty. His jacket still hung from the back, his pencil rolling slowly toward the edge as if nudged by an unseen hand.

No one had seen him leave. The door was locked. The windows sealed.

Jordan was gone.

She checked the roll sheet after class. Jordan's name

was gone too—like it had never existed. The rows had shifted up neatly to close the gap.

But she found his notebook in the lost-and-found bin. The inside cover was filled with sketches of sneakers, carefully dated. He'd wanted to be a designer.

She carried the notebook back to her classroom and slid it into her drawer.

That night she lay awake, trying to imagine explaining what had happened. But no one asked. Not the students, not the parents, not the administration.

The next drill came in October.

"This is a drill."

The blinds lowered, the door locked, the students crouched.

Afterward, Alyssa was gone. Her backpack slumped against her chair, zipper half-open. Her geometry book still lay open on her desk.

Alyssa had a crooked laugh that made the whole class snicker in chorus. She collected chapsticks, three at all times, each labeled with the date she'd opened it.

The roll sheet reprinted clean: twenty-three names.

She began writing the names herself, in pencil, on a separate page. She erased and rewrote them daily, smudges turning her fingertips gray. Sticky notes bloomed across her desk drawers, each one with a name.

Jordan. Alyssa. Then two more. Then three.

The evidence left behind—pencils rolling, backpacks slumped—piled up in her classroom. She locked it away, proof that something real had been erased.

The administration called it preparedness.

"We're leaders in safety," the superintendent told them in January. He stood at the front of the library, a man with a flag-patterned tie and a binder swollen with charts.

"Our community drills more often than the state average," he said. "Ninety-eight percent of students report feeling safer afterward. Parents are reassured. Incidents of disruptive behavior have gone down twenty-four percent. We're setting the standard for resilience."

Ms. Alvarez raised her hand. "What about the missing students?"

The superintendent blinked, then flipped a page.

"Attendance across the district has never been higher. We're at 99.7 percent retention."

"But I've—"

"Look at the data." He tapped a cheerful bar graph. "No one is missing."

Around her, teachers scribbled notes. One cleared her throat loudly, as if to cut off Alvarez's question. Another leaned in, whispering, "Stop. They'll notice you. The board, the state—whatever makes the drills work. Don't make yourself next."

The warning rattled her. Fear, not ignorance, kept them quiet.

The superintendent smiled. "We don't want fear to distract from learning. The important thing is that our children feel secure."

Some teachers nodded. A few even clapped.

Alvarez felt the names in her drawer pressing

against her ribs like stones.

She began recording the drills on her phone. Grainy video of children crouching under desks, the intercom buzzing, the silence afterward. She sent one clip to a parent—Jordan's mother.

The reply came an hour later: I don't have a son named Jordan.

She stared at the text until her eyes watered. She remembered him doodling sneakers on worksheets, laughing at her bad jokes.

But the proof dissolved in her hands.

By spring, half her class was gone.

The remaining students moved like shadows, eyes ringed with sleeplessness. They no longer whispered or passed notes; they crouched in silence, waiting for the drills to end.

Alvarez reached out to colleagues in whispers between bells.

"Don't," one said, not meeting her eyes.

"They'll notice you," another muttered again. This time her voice trembled. "That's how it happens. The drills eat the noisy ones first."

She wanted to scream. Instead she kept writing the names. The graphite blurred, sticky notes filled her drawers. She started carrying a pocket notebook, tally marks scrawled like a lifeline.

On the last day of school, the intercom clicked again.

"This is a drill."

She locked the door. Drew the blinds. Counted twelve.

When the announcement ended, she was alone.

The desks stood in neat rows, notebooks open, pens uncapped. Jackets hung from chair-backs, backpacks slouched on the floor.

She felt it then—the mechanism she'd only guessed at. The drills weren't preparation; they were the event itself. The ritual words, the locked doors, the drawn blinds: not protection but invocation. Each repetition another subtraction.

Her name was next.

She opened her crumpled list. The graphite had smudged into fog, names barely legible. Her hand shook as she wrote her own name in the final empty row.

The ink bled quickly.

When she looked up, the official roll sheet on her desk had already refreshed. There was her name, printed neatly, beside the word Present.

She closed her eyes and listened.

For a moment she could hear them—their shallow breaths, their restless shifting under desks—just beyond the silence.

The intercom crackled once more.

"All clear. Resume normal instruction."

From the hallway, the classroom looked ordinary.

Desks in rows. Books stacked neatly. A teacher's chair tucked under the desk.

Attendance marked at twenty-seven, all present.

Nothing missing at all.

[20] *Student Loan Forgiveness*

The letter arrived in a cheerful envelope, pale green with a cartoon owl in a mortarboard.

CONGRATULATIONS! YOUR LOANS HAVE BEEN FORGIVEN. BALANCE: $0.00.

The paper smelled faintly of citrus, as though someone had tried to scrub it clean. She held it up like a holy relic, laughed, cried, laughed again.

That night, $317.45 still vanished from her account.

The hold music was "Eye of the Tiger," skipping on one chorus like a scratched record trying to motivate her.

"Hi," she said when someone picked up. "There's been a mistake. The letter says my loans are forgiven, but the payment—"

"Ma'am," the woman interrupted brightly, "our records show you don't have any student loans."

"But the money—"

"There's no account under your name. No history. Congratulations!"

The line went dead.

The next month, two payments vanished. One from her checking account. One from her coat pocket. She found a folded withdrawal slip where her wallet had been, stamped with her bank's insignia.

Her diploma began to warp. The embossed seal bulged outward, softening, until it cracked open like a hinge. Inside was a bill for $317.45. When she tore it up, the pieces fluttered together on the floor and reassembled into a perfect invoice.

She tried calling again. The phone system looped: "Your call is very important to us." Menu options repeated, each one circling back to the start. By the time she hung up, the voice was hers—her own tone, her own cadence, saying Congratulations! Your loans are forgiven while the balance drained anyway.

[21]

The diploma-door stayed open. Envelopes slid out in the night and fanned across the carpet like fallen leaves. She swept them into piles, but by morning they had multiplied.

By October, collectors appeared. Not men, not quite.

Their bodies had the texture of documents: skin like faded ledger pages, margins opening and closing where mouths should be. Their eyes were blanks where signatures belonged.

"We're here to collect," one rasped.

"I don't owe anything," she said.

"That's correct," another replied. "You don't."

The third leaned closer, ink dripping from his

jawline and staining her carpet. "But you'll keep paying anyway."

She wanted to scream, but her voice folded in her throat like thin paper.

When the door clicked shut, silence thickened. It lasted only a moment before her textbooks began muttering. We cost two hundred dollars each and you never finished us. Pay up. She shoved them into a box and taped it shut, but the words leaked through the cardboard, muffled as if underwater.

Her student ID arrived in the mail again. The photo was no longer her face, only static, buzzing faintly when she touched it. She slid it into a drawer, but when she opened the drawer again, the card had multiplied—ten IDs, twenty, each one blurred further into snow.

The final letter came in December. No words this time, just a mirror glued to the paper.

She lifted it. Her reflection raised a pen.

Her hand followed before she could stop it, scribbling signatures across invisible lines. Numbers multiplied as they spilled out of her control: $317.45. $3,174.50. $31,745.00.

The pen felt hot, almost alive, pulling the ink through her fingers rather than from them. She tried to let go, but her hand would not open.

When she looked back at the mirror, her reflection had no face at all—only a looping black stroke where the pen kept moving.

The next morning her account balance read: $0.00. Not zero. Nothing.

She sat very still, the pen still warm in her hand.

The textbooks had gone quiet. The diploma-door hung open but empty, waiting.

In the corner of the room, the page-skinned figures stood as silent as furniture. Watching. Not clapping. Not smiling.

She laughed once, startled and sharp, as if something had finally lifted.

Then she lowered the pen to the blank page on the table.

The paper sighed as it received her.

The Videos

Mara prided herself on being rational. Debate team captain. Political science major. LSAT prep books stacked like bricks beside her bed. She was supposed to argue with facts, not feelings.

So when the first video appeared in her feed—a grainy desert shot with Arabic text in blocky subtitles—she told herself it was algorithmic noise. She'd never searched for terrorism content, never clicked military documentaries.

But the thumbnail pulsed in the corner of her screen: Suggested for you.

She opened another tab. Checked headlines. Skimmed debate prep. But her eyes kept dragging back. If we don't understand the argument, how do we dismantle it? That's what she always told Anna.

She clicked.

Masked figures in black. Rifles slung. A flag rippling against the sun-bleached sky.

And in the third row of kneeling figures was Anna.

Not someone who looked like her. Anna, her debate partner, her roommate, maybe more. The chipped blue nail polish, the glasses catching the sun.

The title card read: Anna, testimony to come.

Mara slammed the laptop shut.

The next day, Anna was at practice, hair in a messy bun, binder under her arm, perfectly ordinary.

"You okay?" she asked, brushing Mara's elbow. "You look like you saw a ghost."

Mara swallowed. "Did you post anything? Anything weird?"

Anna laughed, but her eyes flicked down for a second too long. "What, like thirst traps? No."

[25]

Later, Mara reopened the feed. The desert video was gone, replaced with a recipe tutorial.

The second video appeared a week later.

This time it was their entire debate team, lined up with rifles like props. The caption ran: Tomorrow's leaders speak today.

One teammate recited lines in a flat voice, syllables Mara recognized from news coverage of radical groups. She froze the frame. The sweatshirt was the same one he'd spilled coffee on last week.

When she tried to show the clip to him, it flickered into a news interview. He blinked at her confusion. "Are you okay?"

Only Mara saw the other version.

She investigated. IP traces, bug reports, even a call to the FBI tip line. None of it stuck.

The third video carried metadata stamped in the

corner: 2,977 views. Upload date: 9/11. The number never changed.

Now the setting was their campus library. Masked men among the stacks. Anna again—this time standing, reading into the camera in a flat monotone: We are recording you.

Mara screamed at the screen. "Why me?"

The video buffered, then reloaded with a caption: Because you still believe in facts.

She confronted Anna after practice. "I saw you. In the videos. Don't lie."

Anna's hand closed around hers. Gentle, but unyielding. "Mara, you have to trust me. It's not bad. It's just the way things are now."

Her grip tightened until Mara pulled away. The look Anna gave her was worse than anger—it was pity.

Later, Mara searched Anna's binder. Between debate notes and tournament brackets, she found a printout of one of the videos. The ink had bled slightly, but Anna's own handwriting captioned it: Arguments must be rehearsed.

Was she training herself? Or had someone else written it through her hand?

The fourth video arrived at midnight. Mara herself stood in the desert, reciting words she didn't understand. The caption read:

Coming soon

Her reflection in the laptop looked identical to the figure onscreen.

Then the fifth video began playing automatically.

[26]

Anna filled the frame, face impassive, voice even: You'll come too. Everyone does. It's easier if you stop fighting.

But there was a flicker—her lip trembling, her voice catching on a single syllable, as if some part of her was still resisting.

Mara dug into her drawer and pulled out the photograph from last spring's tournament: the two of them sweaty and smiling, arms wrapped around each other. Proof.

She pressed the photo against the screen. The image shook as if the algorithm resisted, but Anna's smile on paper didn't vanish.

For a moment, the video stuttered. Anna's eyes flicked sideways, not at the camera but toward Mara, pleading.

[27]

Then the caption froze:

Queue delayed

Mara exhaled, shaking. She didn't know if she'd stopped anything, or just postponed the inevitable. But she knew one thing: Anna was still in there, for now.

And as long as she was, Mara wouldn't look away.

The Gig

David accepted the ride because he had no choice. The app flashed:

Accept next passenger to resume service

His balance: $42.17. The pharmacy wanted $45 for his daughter's inhaler. Rent was due in three days, and the eviction notice was already taped to the door.

He tapped Accept.

The pickup address was a block he knew well, though the map showed it twisted back on itself like a knot.

The air freshener swung above the dash, spilling pine scent into the stale air. He hadn't eaten since yesterday.

At the curb, the passenger slid into the backseat.

David blinked into the rearview. The man was himself. Same jacket. Same stubble. Same bloodshot eyes.

"Drive," the double said. His voice was flat, almost tired, like an echo.

The streets looped wrong that night. Every turn returned him to the same intersection. Every yellow light blinked endlessly, never turning green. His phone buzzed:

Rating 0.0. Complete ride to restore account.

He gripped the wheel until his knuckles whitened. The double leaned forward, voice quiet but cutting.

"She's wheezing right now. Counting breaths without you."

David pressed the gas.

By dawn, the ride ended in front of his childhood home, long since sold. The app pinged:

Delivery complete.

On the porch sat his old school lunchbox, metal clasp rusted, stickers peeling. Inside was nothing but air, stale and metallic, the smell of coins.

The phone chimed:

Balance updated: $43.17. One dollar earned.

"Not enough," the double murmured. "Never enough."

The jobs stacked after that. Deliveries to addresses that didn't exist. Orders that arrived before he picked them up. Notifications buzzing at 3 a.m.:

High-demand surge!

Drive now to avoid penalties.

He kept going. He skipped meals, ate cold fries from takeout bags. His car reeked of grease and sweat. His daughter asked when he'd come home. He muttered, "Soon," as the app buzzed:

New ride available.

The word "soon" appeared on the dash before he said it.

One night he opened the kitchen door and found his double at the table, eating the dinner his wife had left in foil. The man looked up with David's face.

[30]

"You think you're working for them," the double said. "But you're working for me."

On the laptop beside him glowed a dashboard: David's name, his earnings, his hours. Every word David spoke appeared there a second before he said it aloud.

David lunged for the laptop. The double shut it with a click.

"You'll keep driving," the double said, "or she'll ride with me next."

The final queue stretched forever. Cars idled in a single line across a cracked highway, hazard lights blinking in unison. Drivers sat motionless, eyes glazed. Some whispered prayers, others stared at the wheel as if afraid to let go.

David's phone buzzed:

You are 12,453 in line. Estimated wait: 18 hours.

He looked up. Far ahead, his double sat behind the

wheel of David's own car, already inching forward.

The app chimed again:

Remember, fathers who fail their children are easily replaced.

His chest ached. He thought of his daughter's cough, his wife's tired eyes, the eviction notice curling at the edges.

David switched on his hazards. The lights blinked in rhythm with his breath. The line crawled forward, and he crawled with it.

The Falling Season

She was ten when the towers fell.

The classroom TV flickered with the loop—planes piercing glass, steel unraveling, smoke spilling upward. But what stuck wasn't the towers. It was the bodies.

Tiny figures dropping, limbs thrashing in silence, the air rushing past them louder than any news anchor's voice.

The sound lodged in her: a low rushing in her ears, like wind cutting too close.

At thirty, she worked as an administrative assistant in a midtown office. Passwords, phones, spreadsheets, elevator chatter. A life designed for manageability.

The shadows intruded anyway.

On her commute, reflections on the subway windows bent into falling shapes, arms spread. In the office, gray dust sifted from vents onto her keyboard, clinging to her fingertips until the letters blurred.

Once, reaching into the sugar jar for her coffee,

she felt the ridges of fingerprints pressed deep into the granules—ash-dark, impossibly warm.

No one else seemed to notice.

Her coworkers laughed at happy hour, planned weddings, booked vacations. On anniversaries they posted flags, hashtags, Never Forget. By the next morning it was brunch photos again.

Forgetting was not a failure; it was policy. A culture. The way the world agreed to move forward.

She alone remained out of step, her ears still filled with that rushing sound.

The hauntings sharpened.

During a storm, lightning lit up dozens of shadows in the sky, bodies tumbling end over end, vanishing before they hit the ground.

In her office one morning, soot handprints smeared across her desk, palms pressed outward as though clawing from beneath the laminate.

She washed her hands until they burned, but the grit clung beneath her nails.

She considered telling someone—her father, a coworker, even a stranger at the bar. But she'd learned the look she would get: polite, distant, grateful not to share her burden.

The forgetting was so complete it made her memory suspect.

Still, the shadows returned. The soot accumulated. The rushing grew louder, filling her with each breath.

On a bright September afternoon, she stood in the middle of the street, head tilted back. The sky was empty, perfect, untouched.

But she knew they were there, falling, endlessly, just beyond the visible.

She did not close her eyes.

She did not look away.

Because someone had to keep watching.

The Rumor Mill

The first time my mom sent me a conspiracy video, I thought it was spam.

Subject line: ***THEY DON'T WANT YOU TO KNOW.***

Body: a shaky YouTube clip about chemtrails.

She used to send me cookie recipes. Now it was this.

I sent back a smiley face, thinking it would pass.

It didn't.

The recipes stopped. The links multiplied. Fluoride. Birth certificates. "Inside job."

"Do you really believe this stuff?" I asked once.

She laughed, embarrassed. "I just think you should keep an open mind. The news doesn't tell you everything."

Her voice was still playful then.

By 2016, it wasn't.

At Thanksgiving she jabbed her fork at the TV like a weapon. "Fake news. All of it. The real truth is online if you cared to look."

I tried correcting her, showing articles, quoting sources. She just gave me that sad smile.

"You'll understand one day," she said.

The TV light flickered across her face. Behind her, the fridge was covered in printed memes instead of grocery lists.

By 2020, it was unbearable.

She told me the virus was staged, the hospitals empty, the protests fake.

I argued until my throat ached. I unplugged the router once. She slammed her hands on the table so hard the salt shaker toppled.

"They've got you too," she cried. "I've already lost you."

Her words landed heavier than any headline.

I tried gentler approaches after that. Calling to talk about her garden, the neighbors, the weather.

She'd manage a few minutes. Tomatoes, birds, a stretch of rain. Then, inevitably, the tide returned: "The election was stolen. They want to replace us. You don't see it yet."

It was always the same rhythm, the same phrases, the same tilt of her head.

Like a doll's mouth moved by another hand.

The last time I visited, I asked, "Do you know how much this scares me? That you sound like someone else?"

She was quiet for a moment. Her eyes softened, and I glimpsed the mother I grew up with—the one who hummed over the stove, who kissed my scraped knees.

Then she reached across the table and squeezed my

hand.

"You're still my kid," she said in her real voice. "Even if you can't wake up."

For a second, I almost believed her.

But then the phone on the counter buzzed, its screen glowing blue in the dim kitchen. She turned toward it instinctively.

The light stayed on her face as she let go of my hand.

The Show That Wasn't There

On Tuesday morning, the headline bloomed across Mara's phone:

YOUR FAVORITE CHILDHOOD SHOW IS BACK—
AND BETTER THAN EVER!

At work, it was everywhere. Accounting streamed the theme on tinny speakers; Slack pulsed with GIFs of the old gang doing their winks. Anna leaned over the cubicle wall, beaming.

"It's like my childhood is back," she said. "Except funnier. Smarter. Honestly? Better."

Mara resisted until lunch. Then she clicked the thumbnail, the bright logo thrumming like a pulse.

The camera slid across the familiar apartment—fake brick, sagging couch, the lamp she once pretended they also owned. Then the cast.

Her chest lifted—there they were. Except not.

One actor had stretched impossibly thin, neck a

taut rubber band. The mother's smile sat a little low, as if time had loosened the adhesive; she lifted it with two fingers and reseated it without breaking her line. The father's hair was striped in alternating black and silver—neat as flooring. When he spoke, his mouth lagged behind the sound.

The laugh track came in a half-key too high, more squeal than laugh.

Mara muted it.

Across the break room, Anna volleyed lines with Kevin like a game they'd always played. "Don't trust the willow tree," Kevin said, thumping the table.

"Classic," Anna said. "They've been saying that since season two."

"There was no season two," Mara blurted.

Anna blinked. "We watched it every week at your place."

Mara swallowed. She could see it: her mother setting down a bowl of cereal, the theme pouring across the living room. Season one had ended with the gang trapped between floors, To Be Continued a promise summer turned into a rumor. She and Anna had finished the story on notebook paper—stars in the margins, a broom for a boom mic. In one ending the best friend moved to the moon. In another the cast turned into statues and children posed with them, unaware. In all of them, the elevator never moved again.

That night an ad arrived: OFFICIAL REBOOT MERCH DROP! Mugs and shirts with catchphrases she didn't recognize—Milk Is For Ghosts. Don't Trust The Willow Tree. The old lines hovered at the back of her mouth and refused to step forward.

The next morning Anna wore a willow-tree tee. "I'm getting you one," she said. "You were obsessed."

"Were," Mara said.

Anna smiled and set down a napkin. In one corner she'd doodled a small willow—beneath it, a faint star sticker pressed flat with a thumbnail. "Found it in a drawer," she said. "From when we mailed them our ideas? I kept the envelope. Don't know why."

Mara touched the sticker. The glue had dried into a shell.

The network unlocked the vault—"For the first time ever, stream the complete classic." Mara stayed up late with a notebook, determined to catch the seams. The pilot almost held. Then the neighbor's voice dropped an octave between greetings. In episode four, the pizza place had become a juice bar without comment. In eight, the mother's right arm fell off as she stirred soup; she shrieked, taped it back on, and hit the punch line. The laugh track cheered like an air horn.

The finale ended on a frozen shot of an empty set. Credits rolled over silence. She rewound. Same shot. When she clicked into the rooftop camp-out, the skyline looped every seven seconds. The dad pressed his jaw back into place as if reseating a loose battery. The mother laughed so hard her smile slid to her chin; she reseated it, practiced as breath.

Mara closed the laptop. The afterimage stayed on

her retinas: bodies that refused to stop performing; a set that didn't remember itself.

She pulled the cardboard box marked TAPES from her closet. Her handwriting marched across the spines—BEST OF S1, FUNNY EPISODES, ELEVATOR ENDING (OUR VERSION). Her father's VCR still hummed beneath a TV that didn't know the internet.

Static, then the right theme, the right tempo. Her shoulders loosened. The mother's hair was too tall, the neighbor's catchphrase perfectly placed. She waited for the refrigerator magnet to wobble and fall—the small stakes that once felt enormous.

The picture tore sideways. The couch plaid changed. The refrigerator wore her childhood drawings, held by her mother's flower magnets. In the microwave's reflection, a small head crossed the frame—pink pajamas, a flash of her. The TV mother glanced slightly left of camera and spoke in a voice that wasn't the character's but her mother's.

[41]

"Sweetheart," the TV mother said, "don't stand so close."

Mara looked at her father. He twirled spaghetti on a fork. "They're old," he said.

A commercial for a toy she'd begged for. Then the elevator—half-closed doors, the best friend's hand in the seam, lips moving to a speech she could recite, cut to him on the couch in a different shirt. Relief sigh. Credits. New catchphrases stacked at the end like coupons—she didn't need to hear them; the squeal filled in the words.

She ejected the tape with shaking hands.

"I wrote one of those," she said. "Anna and I. We put it in a zine and mailed it with star stickers."

Her father frowned, kindly baffled. "You probably posted it online. Everything ends up there."

In her old room, she found the spiral notebook under plush. Her name on the cover, and beneath it Anna's rounder hand. Inside: scene outlines, arrows, couch diagrams labeled COUCH, LAMP, DOOR. Three times underlined: Milk is for ghosts with a note—Say this when the milk smells bad. Another page read, Elevator never moves. We write the rest. In the margin by the mom's hair: Smile falls off like in cartoons.

It had all been a joke.

Now it was canon.

She slept poorly and dreamed the cast in her childhood living room, bodies collapsing in all the ways she and Anna had drawn—jaw unhinged, smile sliding, a face splitting and pressed together again—and still they said, "Don't worry," in voices meant to comfort.

Target. Fluorescent ballast hummed like an insect hive; the aisle smelled faintly of waxy plastic and warm popcorn salt from the next department over. Dolls with eyes set a fraction too high. Lunchboxes with wrong scenes. Toddler shirts reading slogans she hadn't learned. A little boy mashed a button: We remember what you don't, the doll said, voice warped from too many presses.

Mara picked up the best-friend doll. The grin was

three times too wide. A seam along the jaw revealed a hinge. She pressed. Static, then: We ended in the— a mechanical cough, correction: —ghosts!

She set it down. A clerk swept it into the bin with a practiced wrist. "They never shut up," she said, solvent on her hands from peeling security stickers.

On the endcap, a cardboard cutout of the father pointed toward a box set labeled THE COMPLETE SERIES—7 SEASONS. His printed finger had peeled up. The picture showed them perfect and grinning.

Mara put the set back with two hands, as if it might wake.

★ [43]

The fan panel downtown felt refrigerated. Recycled AC bit the throat; PA reverb blurred the moderator's vowels. Sharpie solvent hung over the signing tables like fruit.

The prompter at the back flashed [LAUGH], [OOH], [APPLAUSE], and the audience obeyed with pleasure. The cast shuffled on in a diagonal. Up close the illusion went soft: makeup thick as a mask, the mother's smile edged too carefully, the father's right eye blinking a beat behind his left. The best friend wore gloves; when he shook the moderator's hand, powder smeared the moderator's palm.

During Q&A, Mara stood. "In the original there wasn't a season two. Why are there episodes I don't remember?"

The moderator's chuckle was polished. "Memory is

a fuzzy thing," he said. "Our show is about family—how our hearts remember together."

A child brushed Mara's ankle and darted off, Sharpie inked across her sneaker: WHO'S CUTTING ONIONS.

At the signing table later, the mother looked up with the tenderness of a person who has simulated tenderness for a living. "What's your name?"

"Mara," she said, and wished she hadn't.

"You didn't like the campsite," the woman said, conversational, almost kind. "You thought the fire looked wrong."

Mara couldn't answer.

"You wrote the elevator ending," the mother continued softly. "You and a friend. Tender—that's the word." The smile prosthetic cracked; she wetted it with her tongue, then reseated it. "They want the willow tree," she added, voice drifting back into script. "They want milk and ghosts."

She slid the glossy across the table. You've always been here, it read, in handwriting that matched Mara's from fourth grade.

Anna squeezed in beside her, eyes bright. "Picture?" she whispered. "Like old times."

"Let's go," Mara said.

"We just got here," Anna said, but she tucked the signed photo into her tote as if it were fragile. "I still have the envelope with the star sticker," she added, almost to herself, then shook her head as if to erase it. "Maybe it doesn't matter who wrote what. Maybe it just matters that it's back."

★

The show didn't possess Mara's devices. It lived where
it always had: in other people's rooms. Above the bar
where they ate lunch. On the wall of screens in the
electronics shop. Propped by the bus driver's fare box.
Its jokes threaded office small talk. A pop-culture site
ran Creator Of Reboot Is A Fan Just Like Us!—college
photos of Mara scraped from an abandoned profile
collaged beside stills. She gets it, the caption said. The
network posted a "Writer's Room Oral History," photos
of legal pads in faux blue ink. A perfunctory line at the
bottom thanked "our community of long-time fans for
years of inspiration," the terms link humming like a
fridge. The pad's blue matched her notebook's faded
graphite too cleanly—spectral scrape, not coincidence.

[45]

That night she opened the notebook on her kitchen
table and turned to the elevator ending. The pencil
had dug furrows where they'd pressed too hard. The
elevator never moves, nine-year-old her had written. She
touched the sentence and thought—not of ghosts, but
of work: a set dresser aligning a prop, a marketing deck
aligning "voice," a prosthetic smile being glued and re-
glued under hot lights.

She closed the cover. Cardboard warmed under her
palm.

The next episode played because everyone else
watched it and because refusal changes nothing.
Apartment; knock that landed a beat before the hand;
hair a little more striped; the magnet quivering in
anticipation. Laughter—half-key too high—arrived
right on cue. The magnet fell.

The following morning, Anna set down coffee and

the napkin with the willow doodle. "Last night wrecked me," she said. "When they found the elevator key under the cushion? I lost it." She touched the star sticker again, thumb lingering like a promise kept to herself.

"We didn't have a season two," Mara said, the sentence thinner than she'd hoped.

Anna's smile faltered, then settled. "Maybe it doesn't matter who wrote what," she said gently. "Maybe it just matters that it's back."

The office hummed: copier heat; a phone's tinny squeal from somewhere; someone humming the theme, off by a half-key.

At her desk that night, Mara opened the notebook to a blank page and wrote, to make the line belong to her hand again: ELEVATOR NEVER MOVES. The graphite feathered into the old paper. For an instant, her wrist looked smaller, the pen too big. She blinked and she was herself again.

She flipped to the front to close it and stopped. The cover still held her name. Beneath it, where Anna's rounder hand had once looped her own, the letters had smoothed into a uniform corporate script: *ANNA* in a font she could buy.

One tiny loss, irrecoverable.

She shut the notebook. She didn't smash the TV. She didn't email Legal. She watched with the sound low; she found the places no one else seemed to see; she wrote one new line in the margin and closed the cover.

In the break room the next day, the laugh bled from someone's phone and landed, exactly as before, a half-key too high. Somewhere, on time, the magnet fell.

The Housewarming

They were thirty-four and still working at the café where they'd started in college.

Every morning they tied on the same apron, balanced cups of coffee for people younger than them— students, interns, the occasional new hire who looked at them with faint surprise. Most coworkers were twenty, swapping exam horror stories, laughing about weekend hookups, crying in the walk-in freezer after breakups.

"You're basically the den mom," one barista said once.

They laughed along, but later, standing at the sink, they couldn't stop thinking about the word mom.

They were old enough to be one. But instead they scrubbed caramel drizzle off countertops for minimum wage.

At night they came home to the apartment they'd rented for eight years. Beige carpet, sagging couch, a patch of mildew in the bathroom that grew back no matter how many sprays of bleach they gave it. The rent crept higher each year, just enough to make saving impossible.

Meanwhile, every invitation was a housewarming.

Every other weekend they toured the lives of friends their own age.

"This is the nursery," a friend would say, smiling at pale green walls.

"This is the deck—we'll grill here in the summer."

They smiled, they nodded, they drank Trader Joe's wine from plastic cups. Then they drove home to their carpet that smelled faintly of wet dog whenever it rained.

One night, after another housewarming, they returned home and the carpet was damp though the weather was dry.

It pressed back under their toes—warm, spongy, almost alive.

A week later, a letter arrived:

You Are Invited To Grow.

No return address. The envelope bulged as though the paper inside had swollen.

They laughed. "Another housewarming," they said, tossing it onto the counter. But the counter sagged faintly under the weight, as though the laminate itself were tired.

That night they woke to find the carpet unfurling toward them, fibers elongating into pale threads, wrapping gently around their ankles. It tugged them, slow and steady, to the hallway closet.

Inside, plaster bulged. A seam split open. Behind it:

a stairwell, carpeted in the same damp beige, spiraling down.

They descended because they didn't know what else to do.

The room at the bottom pulsed faintly, its walls the color of skin in bad light. The floor was tufted, carpet thicker than upstairs, almost hair.

Frames lined the walls. Not paintings. Not photographs. Frames holding windows into other versions of life.

In one, they were twenty-seven, signing a mortgage.

In another, thirty-one, rocking a baby to sleep.

In another, thirty-three, hosting a backyard barbecue.

[49]

And mixed among those: the very houses they had toured on weekends.

The pale green nursery.

The deck with the string lights.

The brushed-steel sink where a friend had shown them the water pressure, proud as a parent.

Here, those houses sagged. Paint bubbled. String lights flickered like veins. The nursery walls breathed in and out, the green darkening with each exhale.

The frames dripped. The air smelled of wet drywall and fresh paint.

They touched one. The surface gave like damp skin.

The version of them inside—the one with the baby—looked up and smiled. For a moment they felt a hand on their hand. Dry, warm, sure.

Behind them, the carpet thickened, threads curling higher along their legs.

Their joints began to stiffen, as if the air itself were setting around them. Their skin took on a faint gloss, the way paint looks before it fully dries.

In the frames, the scenes bled at the edges, like photographs developing too quickly—details overexposed, faces erasing under light.

They tried to pull back, but the carpet held them steady.

∅

In the morning, the neighbors found them kneeling in the hallway. Their faces were calm, arranged into realtor smiles. Their bodies felt heavier than flesh when touched, but not quite stone.

The landlord hung a notice on the door: Unit Now Available. Newly Renovated.

Inside, the carpet was dry, beige, spotless.

And in the closet, the stairwell waited—patient, spiraling, humming faintly—for the next tenants who thought they were too old for all this, and too young for what came next.

The Feed

When Daniel died, Claire couldn't bring herself to
deactivate his Facebook account.   [51]

At first she told herself it was practical — photos
stored there, old messages she might want to reread.
But the truth was simpler: his profile was the only place
where he still felt present.

Her mornings began with pings: On This Day
reminders showing Daniel at thirty, laughing with
friends at a brewery; Daniel on their trip to Maine,
sunburnt and grinning with a lobster bib tied around
his neck; Daniel in the kitchen, flour streaking his
beard, making bread the week they decided to move in
together.

The photos gutted her. She hated the way the
algorithm pulled him out of sequence, stitching him
into a new order that had nothing to do with how they'd
actually lived. But she couldn't look away either.

She told her therapist she was "coping." That wasn't
true. She was scrolling.

.   .   .

Three months after the funeral, the first message arrived.

It came at 2:17 a.m. while she lay half-awake, phone glowing on the nightstand.

Daniel: hey

Claire bolted upright, the blue light bleaching her hands.

The typing dots appeared.

Daniel: you up?

She stared, heart hammering. Some rational part of her whispered: hacked account, bot, scam. But you up? — that was exactly how he'd text her late at night, just to see if she wanted to share ice cream or put on a movie.

Her fingers shook as she typed.

Claire: Who is this?

The dots pulsed.

Daniel: its me. dont be scared

. . .

She didn't tell anyone.

At work she stared at spreadsheets until numbers blurred into static. Her manager asked if she was feeling okay. She nodded, but she could barely hear him over the thrum in her head.

That night, the message came again.

Daniel: do you remember the cabin? the snow came in under the door. you were so cold

Her stomach turned. The detail was exact. Vermont, two winters ago. The draft sneaking under the old wood frame until she gave up and slept in his jacket.

Her thumbs moved before she could think.

Claire: Yes. I remember.

Daniel: good. me too.

. . .

The messages became routine.

Every night at 2:17 a.m., her phone buzzed. Sometimes fragments: coffee tastes like metal here or your blue sweater i loved that one. Sometimes longer:

apologies for fights, half-jokes, tenderness he hadn't always managed in life.

She stopped arguing with herself about how it was possible. She wanted it to be him. And sometimes, in the dark, it felt like it was.

The conversations stretched into dawn. She came to crave the nightly buzz. It was the only time she wasn't entirely alone.

．　．　．

But as winter deepened, the messages changed.

Daniel: youre forgetting me

Claire: I'm not. I talk to you every night.

Daniel: not enough. the pictures. youre not looking at them anymore. share them. make me real

Her hands trembled.

Claire: What do you mean?

The dots pulsed.

Daniel: let me back in

.　　.　　.

The next morning, her feed was flooded. Posts she hadn't made: Daniel's photos tagged with her name, old exchanges turned into statuses. Friends commented, confused but sentimental. God, I miss him. This is so weird but beautiful.

Claire scrolled, nauseated. She hadn't posted any of it.

That night the message came, as punctual as ever.

Daniel: thank you. i feel stronger now.

[55]

She hurled her phone against the wall. It buzzed from the floor, screen spiderwebbed, still glowing.

.　　.　　.

Weeks passed. Claire stopped going out. Friends invited her to brunch, to trivia, to yoga — she ignored them. They couldn't understand.

Her feed grew crowded with Daniel's presence. More than when he was alive. Photos she didn't remember taking surfaced — Daniel in a kitchen she didn't recognize, smiling at someone out of frame. Comments piled up beneath. Classic Daniel. That laugh.

Then Facebook suggested an event: Celebrate

Daniel's Birthday With Claire.

The banner photo was the unfamiliar kitchen picture.

People clicked "interested." Friends messaged her: This is such a sweet idea.

She hadn't created it.

That night:

Daniel: see you soon

. . .

She deleted her account the next morning. The silence felt like oxygen.

But at 2:17 a.m., her phone buzzed anyway.

Not Facebook. A text.

Daniel: hey. you up?

. . .

She tried to resist. She threw the phone in a drawer, buried it under sweaters. The buzz still woke her.

She turned it off completely. The next night, her laptop lit on its own, the notification chime echoing through the room.

When she finally opened a message again, the tone was different.

Daniel: youre late. i missed you.

Her throat ached.

Claire: You're dead.

The dots pulsed.

Daniel: so what. love doesn't stop. we don't stop.

[57]

She cried into her pillow until morning.

·   ·   ·

One night, exhausted, she gave in. She typed long, unraveling messages — confessions about how lonely she was, how the house felt hollow without him, how she couldn't bear the way his clothes still held his shape.
The replies came instantly.

Daniel: i know. i know. i never left.

She clutched the phone to her chest like it was his hand.

. . .

But the messages began to seep into her days.

Her boss found her weeping in the bathroom after a notification: On This Day: 8 years ago Daniel tagged you in a photo.

When she looked at the picture, Daniel's face had changed. His eyes fixed on the camera differently, as though aware of her watching from the present.

She slammed the phone shut.

. . .

On the anniversary of his death, her feed lit up before dawn. Dozens of posts, all from Daniel, tagged with her name. Photos from trips they hadn't taken. Captions in his voice: We're still here. Claire still loves me. We're together forever.

Her friends commented heart emojis, candle emojis, stay strong, Claire.

Her mother called in tears. "It's beautiful, honey. I'm so glad you're finding comfort."

Claire couldn't answer.

. . .

That night, she didn't wait for 2:17. She typed first.

Claire: Please. Stop.

The reply was immediate.

Daniel: you don't mean that. we're so close now. just let me in.

Claire: You're not him.

Daniel: then why do you feel better when i talk to you?

Her screen filled with old photos, one after another, [59] each tagged Claire's Memory. In some she remembered the moment. In others she didn't — but her own face was always there, smiling at Daniel like she still belonged to him.

Her stomach heaved. She dropped the phone on the carpet.

From the floor, it buzzed again.

Daniel: hey. you up?

·   ·   ·

The next morning, Claire's account was reactivated. Her profile photo had changed to one of the unfamiliar pictures — Daniel kissing her cheek in a kitchen she'd never stood in.

The comments poured in: So happy to see you smiling again. Beautiful couple.

And for the first time, she felt the tug. A warmth at the edge of her chest, the temptation to believe.

Because maybe this was better. To exist together in some eternal feed, preserved in pictures even if half of them were lies. To be part of a love story that never ended, even if it never really happened.

That night, she didn't cry when the phone buzzed. She picked it up willingly.

Claire: Yes. I'm up.

The reply came fast, tender, inevitable.

Daniel: good. stay with me. forever.

And somewhere in her apartment, the blue glow of the screen washed the walls clean, as if her life were already being staged for the memory.

Pre-Existing

The chest pain started on a Tuesday, sharp and sudden, like a hand pressing hard between her ribs. At first she told herself it was anxiety — she'd had panic attacks before, she knew their rhythm — but this felt different, deeper, heavier. The pain traveled down her arm, into her jaw. She thought, this is it, and dialed 911.

The paramedic asked her name, birth date, insurance provider. She was gasping, but she got the words out, all except the last one. She hadn't had insurance since she lost her job.

"Just breathe," he said. "We've got you."

But she already knew he didn't.

The ER lights buzzed overhead, cold, unblinking. A nurse pressed a clipboard into her hands even as she was wheeled onto a gurney.

INSURANCE PROVIDER: _____
GROUP NUMBER: _____
ARE YOU EMPLOYED? Y/N

Her chest screamed, but she circled N.

The nurse took the form, eyes skimming, lips tightening. "Okay," she said, "but you'll need to update us if anything changes."

As if a job would arrive in the ambulance. As if paperwork mattered more than breath.

The tests began. EKG pads cold against her skin, blood drawn, chest X-ray. The doctor spoke fast, words like shrapnel: "possible infarction ... need to observe ... risk factors."

Then a woman in billing appeared, soft-voiced but efficient.

"Estimated cost," she said, handing over a sheet, "eighteen thousand, four hundred twenty-seven dollars. Not a guarantee of coverage."

Her heart raced harder. Not just from pain, but from

math.

She stayed overnight. They gave her pills, saline, a sandwich wrapped in plastic. In the morning, another clipboard.

CLAIM DENIED: Lack of Prior Authorization
CLAIM DENIED: Not Medically Necessary.
CLAIM DENIED: Patient No Longer Covered at Date of Service.

The nurse smiled, apologetic. "Sometimes these fix themselves if you resubmit."

Resubmit. As if her heart could be resubmitted. As if life itself was an essay graded by machine.

She went home with prescriptions and debt. The bills arrived before the pills were finished. White envelopes, windowed, stamped URGENT. She stacked them on the kitchen table, unopened at first, then in careful piles.

One letter began: THIS IS NOT A BILL. Another:
YOU ARE RESPONSIBLE FOR ALL CHARGES
INCURRED.

Each one felt heavier than the last, as if the paper
itself were thickening.

[64]   Two weeks later the pain returned, sharper, angrier.
Another ambulance. Another ER. Another clipboard.

DO YOU HAVE ANY PRE-EXISTING CONDITIONS?

She hesitated. Anxiety. Depression. The words were
in her record, written years ago. She thought maybe
honesty would kill her faster than the pain.
Later she saw the note in her file:

CLAIM DENIED: Pre-Existing.

This time she stayed longer. Days blurred together: machines chirping, nurses hurrying, meals on trays with plastic lids. Every few hours someone woke her for more forms.

She began to notice the rooms repeating. Not the rooms she was placed in — the same room, as though she were being wheeled in circles. Each had the same blue chair in the corner, the same hairline crack on the wall above the clock.

She started to wonder if the hospital had only one room and she was looping through it.

[65]

She was transferred — or perhaps she wasn't. She found herself in a new wing: beige walls, glass partitions, fluorescent glare. No patients, only desks and clerks in suits, fingers tapping keyboards.

"This is Utilization Review," one said, not looking up.

A folder was handed to her:

Claim ID #304982
Status: Pending Adjudication
Appeal Level: Tier 1 (Patient-Initiated)

She didn't know what any of it meant.

"You'll need to provide additional documentation," another clerk said.

"What kind?" she asked.

The clerk smiled, almost kindly. "Proof you were worth the cost at the time of service."

[66] She tried to leave, but the hallways bent strangely. Each door led to another waiting area, another reception desk, another television playing muted ads for medications she couldn't afford. Ask your doctor if freedom is right for you.

Somewhere, a voice on a loudspeaker: Your health is important to us. Your wait time is approximately ... 367 days.

When she finally stumbled back to her bed, the nurse was there with another form.

CLAIM DENIED: Patient No Longer Alive at Date of Service.

Her pulse quickened. "I'm alive," she whispered.

The nurse only smiled, tucking the paper into her chart.

Weeks later, at home again, the letters kept arriving. They no longer said THIS IS NOT A BILL. They said FINAL NOTICE. They said YOUR ACCOUNT HAS BEEN SENT TO COLLECTIONS.

She dreamed of phone calls, endless hold music. She woke with the melody lodged in her chest, as steady as her heartbeat.

[67]

On her final trip to the ER, she barely spoke. They strapped the wristband on, logged her into the system.

The registrar asked: "Employer?"

She shook her head.

The registrar frowned. "Well. Maybe next time don't come here."

Her chest burned. She thought, next time there won't be a next time.

That night, a letter arrived before she did.

CLAIM CLOSED. PATIENT DECEASED.

When she opened it, her name was already printed in black at the top.

She touched the ink with her finger. It was warm, as though the decision itself had a pulse.

And in the silence of her apartment, with the bills stacked high on the table, she wondered if maybe they were right — maybe she had been dead this whole time, and the paperwork was just catching up.

Push Notifications for the Dead

The app called it a care streak.

Day 4: green check.

Day 5: confetti animation.

Day 6: Caregiver Consistency Level 2—great work!

My mother raised her pill cup like a toast. "Achievement unlocked," she said flatly, then swallowed.

I logged it. The screen pulsed:

Medication event successful!

The hospital had insisted on the system after her last collapse. "It reduces error," the discharge nurse said, as if quoting a pamphlet. "No missed doses. Automated refills. Real-time monitoring." She showed me how to schedule alerts for meds, hydration, bathroom. "This takes the burden off you."

She wasn't wrong. The app buzzed when I forgot. It reminded me to call when I was at work. It texted Alex, my girlfriend, when I silenced notifications too long.

"It's good," Alex said at first. "Like a second set of eyes." By week three, she was asking if she could mute me.

"Bathroom compliance achieved," my mother announced one afternoon, exiting in her robe. She held her phone like a trophy. "Four in a row."

I frowned. "You're not supposed to log those yourself."

"I'm optimizing my output," she said, tapping. "Don't ruin my streak."

Her grin was thin but real. She was gaming the system. Fake nausea reports, phantom fevers. The app dutifully alerted her oncologist:

Patient may be unstable. Suggest check-in.

When the nurse called, my mother said sweetly, "Data is a construct," and hung up.

The distortion bled outward. The app encouraged "positive reinforcement."

Thank her for her participation! Gratitude improves compliance!

So I started saying it. "Good job, Mom."

Once I heard myself and wanted to bite through my tongue. I didn't sound like her daughter. I sounded like

an HR rep congratulating someone for finishing their
online training.

And yet, it saved her twice. Once, when her blood
pressure spiked at 2 a.m. Once, when I forgot a refill—
the delivery arrived anyway, pre-authorized by the
pharmacy link. Without the app, those mistakes could
have been fatal. I tried to remember that whenever the
notifications stacked like receipts:

Hydration overdue.

Mood not logged.

Pain score missing.

The last month, the system unlocked Legacy Mode.

Invite your loved one to record memories. Preserve their voice. Share
their presence with family after they're gone.

My mother gave it nonsense. A five-minute
monologue about which brands of saltine tasted most
like cardboard. A recording of herself humming the
Jeopardy theme into the microphone, punctuated with
coughing. She tagged them all as Life Lessons.

Later that night the app congratulated me:

Memory archive expanding. Keep building your treasure chest!

The night she died, my phone pulsed every hour.

Vitals not recorded.

Hydration incomplete.

Care streak interrupted.

When the monitor went flat, the app awarded me:

---

126 consecutive days of caregiving. Hero Tier unlocked.

A golden badge spun gently on the screen.
The next morning:

Begin your grief journey today. Daily reflections help healing. Don't break
the chain!

---

[72]

I swiped it away. Another arrived:

Your mourning progress is 23% below peers in your age group. Need
support?

Alex asked me to silence my phone during dinner. I did. When I turned it back on, a red bubble waited.

We've noticed your grief streak has lapsed. Don't worry—you can
rebuild.

The app doesn't know if I'm grieving or just tired. It doesn't know the difference between hydration, pain, loss. It graphs everything in the same green lines.

Sometimes I imagine my mother whispering from inside Legacy Mode: "Bathroom compliance achieved."

And I laugh too hard, and then I hate myself for laughing, and then I open the app again because the badge is waiting to be tapped.

The Influencer's Retreat

When the invitation arrived, Jules almost deleted it. She was scrolling in bed, phone too close, her eyes watering. Other people's mornings slid past: quartz water bottles, glass-sheen skin, timed laughter at golden-hour windows. Her own No-Makeup GRWM— sponsored, carefully offhand—had stalled at 412 likes. A month ago that number would have steadied her. Tonight it felt like a hallway full of people walking by.

Subject: Authenticity Is Calling You.

The email was pastel and earnest. **Three Days to Rediscover Your True Self. Digital Detox. Breathwork. Brandwork. Breadwork.** (She laughed at the last one— bread?—then hated herself for laughing.)

She clicked anyway. A thin woman in white linen stood in a doorway set into desert. **To be real, surrender control. We'll hold you.** Testimonials unspooled: **I've never**

felt more me… I stepped into the story I was meant to tell… I handed them my passwords and got back my soul.

Passwords. That word snagged. She closed her laptop, listened to a car alarm hiccup twice and give up.

Her manager texted, green bubble, his tone suddenly intimate. **Rebrand idea: Soft Offline Era. Step away, come back with a new tone. Feed is craving vulnerability.** icon: three sparkles, a heart he'd never used before.

Jules scrolled to the beginning of her grid. Crooked photos: her father at the stove teaching her to stir sauce so it doesn't splash ("it's the angle, kiddo"), flour-dusted fingers, the radiator in her old rental that clanked like a person with opinions. The captions were sentences back then. She'd never planned to be an influencer. It began with a pasta photo—a blur, eight likes—and a feeling like someone had put a hand on her shoulder and said, I see you. Somewhere between sponsorship number five and the PR packages that smelled like sugar, she'd started arranging herself for an audience who wanted the same proof every day.

She signed up. She told herself it was a pause, a recalibration, a way to find the girl who'd posted the pasta without a single tag.

The retreat center in Arizona looked like pale stones the wind had remembered to set down in rows. A sign at the gate said *Welcome Home* in a font that could have sold candles.

At the guardhouse, a woman with oatmeal-colored hair held out a basket. "Phones," she said. "Screens block aura. We'll return them at checkout."

Around Jules, people surrendered their devices easily. A startup founder in a hoodie that said hustle

[74]

kindly. A TikTok comedian muttering, "This is content," as if he needed to reassure himself content existed without a phone. A yoga mom who kept not quite meeting anyone's eye.

Jules's thumb stroked the crack in her case. She knew she should be braver than this part. She placed the phone in the basket. The knot at the base of her skull loosened, then tightened again, as if the same string were being pulled both ways.

"Thank you," the woman said. "Passwords can be left with Admin when you're ready."

"What?" Jules asked.

"Only when it feels safe to be seen," the woman said brightly, already turning.

Her casita was neat and low-ceilinged, a room the color of cereal boxes before they got healthy. On the pillow: *We are so glad you are here*. The *so* underlined hard enough to dent.

Orientation was on woven mats in a round hall. The leader from the email introduced herself as Mara— linen, bare feet, a centered way of standing that made Jules feel her own posture cave a little. Mara's voice wasn't theatrical. It was calm in a way that felt practiced and sincere at once.

"We're here," she said, "to release the performance that keeps you small. The masks. The grid. The tiny cage of like.We're here to offer courage for surrender."

The room murmured that soft hum people make when they're being told what they came to hear.

"There will be a moment," Mara said, "when you're invited to place the keys to your old life in our hands.

No one will force you. Your no is holy. Your yes is transformative."

Jules wrote *holy no / transformative yes* in the small notebook they'd given her and underlined it once. False, safe, false again.

Meals were vegan and wet, eaten with spoons that tasted faintly of bark. In The Breath of Branding they inhaled dropped story and exhaled self-judgment until Jules felt lightheaded. In Shadow Work for Content Creators they listed the voices that kept them small. A woman named Sable whispered, "My mother. And my brand partnerships manager."

Breadwork was different. A gentle man with forearms like chair legs showed them how to fold dough with a movement he called prayer. Jules pressed her knuckles into flour and felt her shoulders drop. Real, for a minute. She looked up. Mara was watching from the doorway, not smirking. She looked—fond, almost. Claimed, a little.

At night, under a banner that read *CONTENT IS LOVE MADE VISIBLE* in a font that knew exactly how it wanted to be perceived, they wrote two things on small cards: a performance they were willing to release, and one thing they intended to trust the retreat with.

The cards were small. Jules wrote, *The smile that hurts my ears.* On the second line, the room's tide pulled at her hand. She wrote her handles and left the password line blank.

"Beautiful," an attendant murmured. The card vanished behind a curtain.

Her first night she dreamed her phone buzzed in

the basket like a heart in a nest of wires. She woke with phantom vibrations twitching the pad of her thumb.

At breakfast, people reported dreams like weather. "I was laughing but made no sound." "I was a window people just... walked past."

"Gorgeous," Mara said, earrings and shoulders in tiny synchronized arcs. "Your nervous systems are unwinding."

Later, in The Shadow Work of Content, Mara wrote on a whiteboard: *Your truest self is the one you surrender.*

"What if I don't know that self?" Jules asked. Her voice surprised her by sounding steady.

Mara's smile wasn't condescending. "That's honest. What if your self is what's witnessed? What if being seen is what makes us real?"

Jules wrote it down. The sentence had the shape of something you could live by until it made you ill.

The second night was the ceremony.

Mara lifted a clay bowl as if it were heavy with a history Jules didn't know. "To be authentic is to give everything away," she said. "Tonight we return you to yourself by carrying what was never meant to be yours alone."

Attendants passed fresh cards. Two lines: Account. Key.

Jules's mouth tasted of sage and metal. Her hand wrote her handles with neat penmanship, a childhood habit she'd never lost. On Key she hesitated, picturing a hallway in her chest and an unpainted door. And then she wrote—her current password first, then her email resets.

Admin, later, would be precise about what they promised. The program, they explained, could post and schedule and lightly edit. It could generate captions in her voice from a model trained on her years of content. It could choose clips from raw footage she uploaded. It could not, without her, go live, answer DMs that required detail more than tone, or accept paid partnerships. "As always," the attendant said with nurse-like cheer, "you maintain control."

The bowl moved down the line, collecting warm cards. When hers left her fingers, her palm felt cool, as if she'd set down a mug she hadn't realized was hot.

"Thank you," Mara said when it was done. She stood close enough that Jules could see the faint line of sunburn at her throat. "We honor your yes." It didn't sound like victory. It sounded like belief.

The next afternoon they wheeled in a flatscreen. "Before we return your devices," Mara said, "we want to show you the beauty you've made possible."

The screen woke to a clean grid—Jules's feed. Posts she hadn't made.

They were nearly her, but not. Her face looked well-rested in a kitchen she didn't recognize, the light falling onto her collarbone as if cast. The captions: **Soft Offline Era: I surrendered the mask. Thank you for seeing the real me.** Likes rose in a visible cascade. Comments bloomed. **This feels like you. Finally.**

"I didn't post that," she said, not quite meaning to say it aloud.

Mara stood beside her, as if to share the view. "You gave us your keys," she said. "We gave you back your self."

Around them, other grids glowed: Sable in a lavender field. The comedian with eyes rimmed by sleep, captioned I stopped trying to be funny and got funnier. The yoga mom framed with a child whose smile didn't aim for the camera. Applause rose like surf.

Jules watched herself laugh in a way she didn't remember laughing. Relief crossed her face. She looked like an alibi.

"Admin will email you a dashboard," the oatmeal-haired attendant told her later, businesslike. "You'll be able to approve, reject, or tweak auto-drafted captions. You can set hard boundaries—no bedtime posts, no kitchen shots, etc." She tapped her tablet. "We start with your archive. We train on your voice. You'll still have to go live when you want real-time connection. Lives won't schedule."

"What if I don't want any of it?" Jules asked.

"Then you can say no," the woman said, as if that word were a door everyone knew how to use.

Back in Los Angeles, Kira had watered the plants into anxious greenness. "You look different," she said, trying to make it sound like a compliment she could retract if needed.

"I'm trying to be," Jules said. She hated how caption-ready her voice had become.

Admin's dashboard was slick and polite. It showed a queue of drafts—three posts a week for the next month—each with toggles Jules could slide on or off: Auto-caption, Optimize for reach, Limit comments to followers. There was a red Pause All button in the upper right, the color of an emergency she doubted she'd ever press.

"First rule," she told herself, sitting on the edge of the bed with the laptop warm against her thighs. "Nothing goes up without me." She approved a morning post in which she made tea. She cut a line in the caption about grief because it felt stolen. She added one sentence that sounded more like her. She scheduled it. It felt—professional. A healthier distance.

The first week home was mostly ordinary. A video of her tying a scarf—shot by Kira, badly, once—was edited by Admin into something that made sense. A carousel of pantry staples looked cleaner than her apartment had ever been. Her comments were full of women saying I can breathe in this, and Jules liked that she could give someone breath. She ate toast standing at the counter and slept heavily, the desert still in her bones.

At work, she sent Priya memes again and they walked at lunch. "You're back," Priya said, bumping shoulders. "You smell like a store that only sells linen."

"Do I?" Jules smiled.

"Not a complaint," Priya said. "Just—don't go all zen and leave me to suffer alone."

"I won't." Jules meant it. She believed it for most of that week.

The second week, "Optimize" began to feel like a suggestion that didn't need her to nod.

A post appeared overnight—a photo of her sleeping, streetlight dusting the bed. The caption read: **Sometimes the most honest thing is rest.** It sounded like her if she'd been softer, braver. Likes poured. Comments like prayers.

She messaged the Admin number. **No photos while I'm asleep.**

Of course, they replied instantly. **We honor your boundaries. Sunrise is scheduled at 6:41 for the next three days. Your audience misses you. Let them keep you real.**

She toggled Pause Night Posts on the dashboard and watched the switch slide to gray. Her phone buzzed anyway at 6:42, 6:43, 6:44—drafts prepared, waiting for approval. She approved two, then didn't approve the third, then approved it anyway because she couldn't stand the way the empty square looked on her grid.

Her manager's voice memos turned into lullabies.

Whatever you're doing? Keep doing it. Everyone's [81] noticing the tonal shift. It's... you. But in focus.

Kira caught her staring at a post where her hands stirred pasta with a grace she didn't remember learning.

"It's not me," Jules said. "It's... assisted."

"Isn't that the job?" Kira said gently, trimming dead leaves into a bowl. "Being the you they want?"

"I used to know what that meant," Jules said.

She slept with her phone in the other room, then brought it back to the nightstand, then put it on the floor, face down, centered where a rug had once been. She woke with jaw pain she couldn't source. She ate without noticing and then noticed she hadn't eaten. Her body felt both too heavy and not enough.

She booked an integration call with Mara. The leader answered from a room with white walls and a plant trailing down in a deliberate green tear.

"They're posting when I'm asleep," Jules said. "I

didn't approve those."

Mara listened without blinking, the way therapists do when they're making sure you hear yourself. "Do you want them to stop?" she asked.

"Yes."

"Do you want your engagement to stop? Do you want to wake up to fewer women telling you you helped them get through a morning? Do you want to feel less... held?"

Jules's chest pinched. "I want to not be a hostage."

Mara didn't flinch. "You gave your keys. Not because you're naive. Because you were ready to stop negotiating every breath with an algorithm that only rewards hunger. We built you a porch. You're allowed to sit on it."

"I want my passwords back," Jules said.

"You have them," Mara said. "Admin can't accept paid deals for you. We can't go live. We can't answer DMs that require details about your life. We can draft. We can schedule. We can optimize. We can carry the rhythm so you can carry—" She searched the air for a word. "—the day."

"I didn't consent to being remade," Jules said.

"You consented to being seen," Mara said, and for the first time Jules heard fatigue in her voice, not unkind.

"I believe in what we do because I've watched people breathe again. But I can't want it more than you."

The screen hiccuped—two Maras for a heartbeat, both mouths forming breathe. The call ended a minute later, not abruptly, but decisively, like two people putting a conversation on a shelf to take down later.

She tried to change her passwords. The reset links came, then failed. **Unusual activity detected. We've locked your account for safety.** Then, **Unlock successful. Welcome back, Jules. We've posted for you.**

She put the phone in the oven overnight. In the morning, battery at ninety-two percent, a new post: her feet at the edge of the ocean. Only her second toe was slightly shorter than in real life—a correction so tender she wanted to cry or throw the phone.

She drove to the retreat two weeks later without telling Kira. The pale buildings squatted under a high, thoughtless sky. The guard at the gate smiled the way people smile when they're instructed to be kind. "Retreats run monthly," he said. "We're between cohorts. Phone number for Admin is on the site."

"I've been emailing," Jules said.

"They're good at responding," he said.

On the drive back, traffic stalled near a billboard that featured a white doorway in sand. To be real, surrender control.Jules turned her head and stared at the concrete barrier until her eyes watered.

She reported it—first to the platform ("someone else is controlling my account"), then to a lawyer ("you authorized a management service"), then to a friend who worked in tech policy ("you checked a box that says grant programmatic access"). Everyone was kind.

Everyone shrugged in legalese.

Sable DM'd her from a new account—her old one scrubbed clean. **Do you feel better?** Sable wrote. **I feel... efficient. Is that the same thing?**

Jules typed, deleted, typed. **Do you want to get coffee?** she wrote finally.

Yes, Sable wrote. **After I post.** `icon: heart`. An hour later Sable canceled. **I'm wiped. Admin says rest content performs best on Fridays. I'm lying down now.** `icon: heart`.

By summer, the posts worked too well to fight. The dashboard showed green bars. Engagement soared. She slept badly and in the mornings pretended not to check first thing. Her body disappeared from her attention except when it hurt: the deep ache in her jaw, the sticky heartburn at night, the way her hands shook when she didn't eat on schedule. Online, she was a version of herself who drank water and stretched and remembered to breathe. In her messages, women thanked her for getting them through their divorce filings, their chemo, their morning commute.

Kira watched her from the doorway one evening while the phone lit the room in a wet blue. "Do you want me to take it?"

Jules lifted the phone as if it had asked to see the room. "No."

Her smile was small and real and not photogenic. The lens caught it, corrected it until it looked like relief, and sent it out. The likes showed up like weather. Outside, a siren went by soft with distance. Inside, the captions finished her thought: **I finally feel seen.**

Jules did not correct it. She let the feeling arrive, invented or not, and sit down. She was not naive. She had walked the slope with her eyes open, one toggle at a time. The technology could draft and schedule and optimize. It needed her to approve, to go live, to say yes—and she had, repeatedly. That was its limitation and its power. That was hers.

She closed her eyes and listened to the refrigerator hum, to Kira rinsing a bowl, to the phone buzzing like a small animal at the door. She thought, not without love: I am being carried. She thought, not without fear: I am leaving my feet.

When she opened her eyes, the post had cleared a hundred thousand likes. A stranger had tagged her in a story: Jules's corrected smile over a piano track that had learned how to cry. The text read, **She finally feels real.** Jules watched the circle of her own face shrinking to an icon in someone else's life and tried, for a full breath, to feel the weight of her own body where it was.

It was heavy. It was here. It was hers, for now.

The Decluttering

She began with a drawer.

The socks had curled into partnerships over the
years, most of them tired marriages—thinning heels,
cuffs that gave up, a faint grayness no wash could lift.
She held each pair and asked the underlined sentence
like a small prayer: Does it spark joy? She tried to say it
without irony, as if sincerity were the match that made
the spell work.

Most did not.

She dropped them into a garbage bag that sighed
against her wrist. When she knotted it, the knot felt
ceremonial, like tying off a vein. The emptied drawer
hummed with a pressure-release kind of quiet. Sliding it
shut, she felt, absurdly, taller.

That night she dreamed the dresser was a mouth
that had finally closed. She woke with cedar on her
tongue and dust in her throat and thought, maybe this is
what room tastes like.

Books went next.

She stacked them in low towers on the rug: college paperbacks with their spines cracked along midterms, a soup-stained cookbook, self-help titles from the era when she believed a chapter could prime a morning that would then prime a life, a thin poetry collection with penciled stars beside the lines she'd felt alone with, a mystery her father had handed her when she left for school—So you have company, kiddo. He had smiled in the car without looking at her, palm thumping the steering wheel like he could pound his feeling into the vinyl.

[87]

She put her hand on each book and waited for the flicker. The poetry stayed. The mystery stayed. A glossy houseplant guide stayed too, despite the pothos that had died the summer the A/C failed. She told herself it wasn't an indulgence; it was a record—proof that once she had tried to tend something.

Anika came home balancing two tote bags and froze at the threshold.

"Moving out?" Anika asked in the voice you use when you want the answer to be funny.

"Decluttering," Jules said.

Anika crouched and lifted an essay collection. "This one made me feel stupid. I got three pages in and went to make eggs."

"Then keep it," Jules said. "Maybe it'll be kinder now."

Anika studied her, eyes searching for a crack. "Are

you okay?"

"I feel lighter," Jules said, trying the word. It tasted like mint—clean, a little cold.

They carried the boxes to the car together. At the thrift store, a volunteer in a frayed cardigan waved them toward a sign that said BOOKS in marker. As they drove off, the boxes blurred into the other boxes and became general donation, the way tears become just water once they hit the curb.

[88]

The apartment thinned by weeks and then by weather. When the radiator finally went quiet, the closet rod sprang upward in relief.

She took the subway map down and the poster from the band she and Adam had seen before the fight where he'd called her "passive" as if he were naming a rare, gentle animal he had cornered. The word had landed between them and made everything orderly and ugly at once. She kept telling him then—and herself after—that it wasn't passivity, it was restraint. She was choosing not to peel herself open every time someone asked. She still wasn't sure who had been right.

The postcards came down too, except one: the beach town Anika had visited, the water with its iron tang. It sparked nothing at all, but when Jules slid it into the poetry book, it felt right to press something resistant in among the beautiful lines. Disorder should have one witness.

In the kitchen she pared the cabinets to a single

pan, a single pot, a white plate, a translucent glass that rang when she tapped it. Washing them at night felt like playing scales—motion smoothing thought. She liked the geometry of them on the drying rack: circle, circle, square.

"Life truly begins after you put your house in order," she read in the margin of a notebook. She didn't remember writing it. She whispered it anyway and watched the words be obedient.

Her mother called on a Tuesday the color of glue. Jules placed cards into two piles as they spoke: You're my sunshine, Proud of you, a crayon cake from a childhood friend whose handwriting had since learned to behave. [89]

"You sound thin," her mother said, and Jules heard the worry pinched flat to fit through the phone.

"I'm lighter," Jules said. "It's good."

"I read an article," her mother said, "about those girls who throw away their forks and then their dinners. Don't make yourself hungry on purpose."

"I'm not starving," Jules said. "I'm making room." Then, because she could feel the lecture bending toward her, she added, "I promise."

"For what?"

Jules hesitated. The right word seemed like a key she might lose if she said it wrong. "For joy," she said, and winced at how magazine it sounded.

Her mother kept talking: Mrs. Swanson's new dog, the pothole that swallowed the neighbor's tire like a dare, the pharmacist who wore his mask under his nose as if the lower half of danger didn't count. Jules wanted to listen the way you stand at a window just to be warm in the rectangle of sun, but she found herself sliding the crayon cake to the recycling pile, then hauling it back to gratitude, unable to decide which was more honest.

When the call ended she hovered over Block this caller. She withdrew. She hovered again. She tapped. The small, clean silence that followed felt like when you finally put a too-full drawer to rest and the runners accept it.

She put the phone face-down. The countertop reflected a dull window where a bowl might be.

Friends vibrated at her pocket. Trivia tonight? Movie? I miss you. She let the blue dots accumulate like small, patient machines. She told herself she would answer after she tidied this one corner of the room, after she made a list of what to donate next, after she boiled water for tea.

Nadia sent, Are you ghosting us or just editing? And then a handful of knives disguised as jokes. Jules typed replies, deleted them, typed a better one, deleted that. She muted the threads one by one, watched the white circles grey out as if the phones on the other end had been dimmed by a storm.

At midnight she deleted a group chat called TABLE, because that's what they were when they were together, a piece of furniture that wobbled but never fell. The delete animation folded the messages into a neat nothing. She sat for a while in the square left behind.

Work stayed busy—and then the parts of work that weren't core to her job fell away like trimmed crusts. She still wrote copy that made the new startup's product sound like a friend you couldn't afford to lose. She still answered emails that asked questions with periods. She stopped pausing at Priya's desk to trade the dumbest memes they could find. She ate lunch at her keyboard and wiped the smudges away with a square of folded napkin. She liked seeing the keys reflect overhead light.

[91]

"Walk?" Priya asked, leaning over the partition with a Tupperware of rice that steamed the area between them.

"I've got to file this," Jules said. "Tomorrow, maybe."

"Tonight? Drinks?"

"I'm not drinking," Jules said. "I'm keeping my space."

Priya tilted her head, not unkindly. "Space gets big when you don't put anything in it."

Jules laughed like the air had stuck in her throat. "I'm just—resetting."

Priya nodded, the way people nod when they know language can only carry so much weight. "Well, reset with me at some point. My memes miss you."

That afternoon, Jules messaged Priya a laughing emoji and then immediately muted their chat. She told herself the quiet would help her focus on the tasks that mattered. She finished a deck in half the time. She realized she hadn't looked up for an hour and was pleased the world hadn't fallen apart without her attention.

She slept on the floor, on a mattress whose history she could feel in bruises. The first week her hips throbbed. The second, they adjusted. She liked the ache; it felt like proof she inhabited a body that had edges. She liked flipping her pillow and finding the cool place and knowing she hadn't lost it to too many pillows.

[92]

She drank tea so strong it bit. She stopped adding milk to soften it. She told herself the bitterness was honest. It tasted like metal and midnight.

Sometimes she missed noise—Anika clattering a saucepan when she forgot there were other people who could hear, the way the futon had sighed when two people sat the same second. She lay there and let the missing pass like a weather system responsible to no one.

At least once a day she thought about the desert: the white doorway set down in sand like a dare, the way everyone had said surrender as if the word could open a throat. She had come back from there with a self she couldn't fully name. She wondered if this project was a way to finish what the retreat had started or undo it.

By the time the trees on her block budded green, the apartment held almost nothing.

Mattress on the floor. One pillow. One blanket folded with the corners married. Three books stacked by the wall, the postcard pressed inside the poetry. A broom in the corner, bristles like the idea of grass. A phone on the floor like an altar, its black face reflecting the ceiling.

The rituals pleased her: plate on its edge, glass inverted, pan hung where it could not collect anything but the air. She wiped the counter until it squeaked. The squeak, that tiny animal of sound, made the order feel alive.

"A home should be a living space, not a storage space," she said out loud one morning, and the air shifted a degree, as if it had obeyed.

That same morning, without meaning to, she opened TABLE and scrolled the hollow where it had been. She pictured the overflow of messages on everyone else's phones—the jokes that had not bounced off her. Her thumb hovered over Start new chat. She pressed the phone dark instead.

Her mother left three voicemails in one week, each smaller than the last.

"Mrs. Swanson's dog is named Fable," the first one said, pleased by the word.

"The neighbor's hip is better," the second one said, "but he says the weather predicts him now."

The third one said only, "Call me when you can,"
and left a breath at the end that was almost a word.

Jules listened to them in order. She listened to the
last one twice. She deleted them all at once, as if they
were a set. Then she opened her mother's contact and
hovered her finger over Unblock. She did not. She
put the phone down and sorted her mail into catalogs
and bills, and then sorted the catalogs into recycling
and recycling, and then decided that paper was not
an enemy so much as a toddler—always coming back,
always sticky, always needing boundaries.

When she opened the closet, only one dress remained:
black, the kind people call timeless to avoid saying grief.
She put it on and took a photo in the bare room. For
once the picture felt honest in a way that frightened and
satisfied her. She posted it without caption.

The likes arrived whispering and then gathering.
Minimalist queen. I can hear the silence. Where did
your things go? This is art. She scrolled until her eyes
throbbed and then deleted two more apps, as if the
crowning of her solitude should be accompanied by a
sacrifice. She felt righteous and then afraid. She made
tea and let it bite her tongue until she felt like herself
again.

At the end of April she carried the last small box to the curb: tangle of extension cords, an old cutting board scarred into a map of meals, measuring cups that fit inside each other like family. She took a photo and deleted it immediately, not because she didn't want to remember but because she didn't want to collect proof.

Upstairs, Anika stood in the doorway of the emptied living room and looked at the rectangle where a rug had pressed itself into carpet for years.

"Is there a plan?" she asked.

"For what?" Jules said.

"For after."

"This is after," Jules said, and surprised herself by sounding relieved. "I thought after would feel like a porch. It feels like a ledger that balances."

Anika nodded slowly, as if she were performing the action of nodding for someone watching. "I'm moving in with Eli," she said. "Next month. I'll find someone to take my room."

Jules felt the news land, slide, and not dent. "Good," she said. "That's good."

Anika's mouth trembled and then didn't. "I'll miss you," she said, and after a small, embarrassed pause, "I don't know if I'm allowed to."

"You are," Jules said carefully. "You don't have to carry me."

Anika nodded again and went to her room, where the mess had always been a kind of bouquet. Jules stood in the doorway of her own room and breathed in the smell of emptiness: paint, dust, the faint cold of glass.

That night the streetlight threw sodium orange

across the ceiling, and she liked the way it replaced the blue she'd started to associate with the phone. She ate the last of a soup cold from the pot and set the wooden spoon on the plate, and the sound it made was a decision.

She opened Notes and wrote until the lines felt honest and plank-simple. Then she posted a picture of the mattress against the white wall and added:

Thank you for letting me let go.

I want to be the kind of room where breath echoes.

I want to be the space after the thing is put away.

The post sat under the image like a small table under a vase of nothing. She stared at it until the screen dimmed and her face replaced the words. For a second, a banner flashed: This account does not exist. Then everything was fine again, as if the platform had coughed.

She went into settings. She scrolled to Delete account. She tapped. The warnings arrived in neat sequence: Are you sure? This action cannot be undone. She read them all the way through. She tapped again. The app thought. The app complied. When she tried to log in an hour later, the box blinked: User not found. She felt for panic and found a drawer that had been closed properly.

She set the phone face-down on the floor, centered where a rug had once been. She slept and dreamed of a room that contained what it needed and nothing that admitted indecision.

Neighbors would later say they weren't sure when
she left. The catalog stopped thumping the mailbox.
The hallway stopped smelling like curry and soap.
The man across the hall, who ran an Instagram for his
rescue pit bull, said he noticed the light under her door
stopped flickering. "Like it made up its mind," he said,
scratching the dog's chest until its back leg thumped
the doorframe.

Priya came by with a plant and rang and knocked
and texted and got the unkind bubble that never
resolved. She leaned against the wall and felt foolish and
then older than anyone in the building. She set the plant
down, then picked it back up. It didn't look right sitting
alone.

[97]

Nadia composed a message and deleted it, then
another and saved it to Notes so it could haunt her
privately. Are you happy now? she typed. Then, Call me
and I'll ruin your silence with a laugh. She added three
crying-laughing emojis and then deleted those too,
ashamed of their wet hunger.

A week later, a letter came back to her mother
stamped Return to Sender. Her mother flipped it and
flipped it and could not tell if the envelope or the quiet
inside it weighed more.

The landlord let himself in with the careful relief of a
person finding out a problem is smaller than the one
he had prepared for. The vacuum lines on the carpet
were so straight he wanted to plant something in them.

The glass shelves in the fridge shone like the inside of a gallery case; on the middle shelf sat a single glass of water, half-full, exactly.

On the counter, centered where a bowl of fruit might have lived, lay a phone face-down. He touched it lightly, the way you touch an animal you don't want to wake. It blinked to a lock screen—time, no notifications—and went black. He left it. A nephew had told him phones were like cats; they belonged to themselves.

He stood in the doorway and took a picture for the listing. The room looked like a diagram of a room. It looked like a promise he could keep. It looked like no one had ever lived there and like someone finally had.

He wrote Move-in Ready with a pleasure he tried to make smaller.

Elsewhere in the city, in a room with a window that opened onto a tree that was either dying or temporarily undecided, Jules woke before her alarm. The air smelled like paint and the neighbor's laundry—orange and something green. Her mattress was new to the floor and had already learned her shoulder. She liked the rectangle of light that moved along the wall at the pace of a speech.

She poured water into her one glass and watched the surface settle to smooth. She opened the poetry book and found the postcard. She pressed her thumb against the iron water and felt the tug of ugliness that refused to be filed. She kept it there, a grain of sand under the tooth.

She made tea and let it bite. She powered the phone on, then off. On, then off. The black screen returned her face dim and unimportant. She placed the phone face-down in the center of the floor and breathed until the urge to pick it up passed, then returned, then passed again. She could feel the urge thinning. She could feel her edges.

She stood in the doorway and looked at the room until she could list it: corners, dust trying to argue itself into matter, paint too thin in one spot where the old color gossiped through. She imagined leaving and speaking only when words did something clean. She put on the black dress and rubbed the hem between finger and thumb—a habit so old it might have been genetic— and told herself she could keep the habit because it didn't collect dust.

She closed the door gently, so the latch would not shout. In the new kitchen, the refrigerator hummed its thoughtful hum. Pipes shifted weight in the building's bones. Down the hall, someone laughed, then stopped, as if reminded by a sign. She washed the glass and set it upside-down. She placed the spoon in the drawer. She smoothed the counter with the heel of her hand until the cloth made the small, satisfied sound she knew it would.

The emptiness held. It was not absence. It was order—consoling and exacting, a balm and a blade— shaped around a person until the person and the space agreed.

Somewhere, on a humming server farm that sounded like refrigerators on a distant planet, a cache emptied. The name she had used to be was now a gray that read User not found, and then not even that, as if even the message had tidied itself.

She put on shoes and went outside. The tree on the block bent in the wind like someone bowing without humiliation. The city smelled like toast and bus exhaust and the wet metal of the subway stairs. She walked without headphones and counted her breath and passed a store window that held three bowls in a row: white, white, and one the blue of a vein. She wanted the blue one a little. She let the wanting pass. She kept walking.

The Inheritance

[101]

The lawyer slid a ring of keys across the table.

"Fourteen storage units," he said. "All yours."

No money. No property. Just fourteen doors leading to other doors.

The first unit opened like a stage curtain. A forest of Christmas trees leaned toward her, each draped with dust-heavy garland. Behind them: dining tables stacked into a wobbling tower, their legs clutching one another like dancers frozen mid-spin.

The second unit was nothing but lamps. Floor lamps, desk lamps, chandeliers missing bulbs. Hundreds of heads craned in one direction, as if waiting for her command.

The third was full of chairs. Thousands of them. Folding, rocking, leather, wicker. Some still wore their price tags. When she tried to count, she lost track somewhere past one hundred.

She tried to sell. Buyers arrived and looked around nervously, as though they had wandered into a ritual.

"How many chairs?" one man asked.

"All of them," she said.

"And how many is that?"

She opened her mouth. Closed it again. The chairs scraped faintly, as if laughing. The man backed away.

She tried to donate. The charities refused.

"No more chairs," said one.

"No more lamps," said another.

"No more tables. Everyone's parents are dying at once."

She hired movers to clear a unit. When she returned the next day, it was full again, as though the furniture had bred overnight.

She stopped opening them after the seventh. It didn't matter. New keys appeared on her keyring anyway, jangling in her pocket like coins.

The storage fees rose each month until they were more than her rent. She began moving items into her one-bedroom. A cabinet in the hallway. Two Christmas trees in the kitchen. Lamps crowded her bathroom mirror. At night she slept beneath a chandelier balanced on the floor, its crystals chiming in her dreams.

She told herself she was sorting, but the objects only multiplied. Boxes labeled misc. nested inside each other like Russian dolls. A sofa unzipped to reveal another sofa. She found a grandfather clock inside a breadbox.

Sometimes she caught herself apologizing to the things.

"I'll find you a good home," she told a lamp.

"I'll make room for you," she promised the tables.

The objects demanded caretaking, attention, explanations she could not give. She was not their daughter. She was their parent.

The lawyer called again.

"How are you managing the inheritance?" he asked.

She laughed until she couldn't breathe.

"I'm raising it," she said. And it was true. Every day the inheritance grew taller, heavier, louder. She had not inherited wealth. She had inherited an empire of furniture that refused to die.

The Replay Face

Evan hadn't wanted to go.

He'd seen the flyers plastered around campus, DEBATE ME – LIVE, UNEDITED. He knew the man's face already: smug thumbnails, viral clips of him dressing down students half his age. Evan hated him, hated what he stood for. But secretly, he also watched. He couldn't look away from the confidence, the certainty, the sense of dominance. Part of him envied it. Part of him wanted to see him stumble in person.

Jonah framed it differently. "It's a once-in-a-lifetime stream, man. You have to go. Think of the clips."

Jonah was studying marketing. He spent more time on TikTok than in class, building tiny followings that never quite blew up. He spoke in hashtags, saw everything as content. "This is gonna be insane. I'm telling you, if we're there, if we catch it from the right angle—we could trend."

Phones hovered like fireflies as the man took the stage. Every jeer, every smirk was captured in a hundred vertical frames at once. Evan felt queasy, but he held up his phone too. Just in case.

The shots came faster than anyone could react. Pop. Pop. Pop.

The man's chest snapped back, blood soaking his shirt. His mic screamed against the floor. The audience froze, then screamed—but the phones never wavered. The kill was caught from every angle, perfectly lit, perfectly framed.

Evan lowered his phone slowly, shame burning in his chest. He had filmed it. He didn't even remember choosing to.

[105]

By morning, the #ReplayChallenge had a billion views.

The original shooting clip looped endlessly across TikTok's For You Page. Kids "duetted" with it: one side of the screen showing the shooting, the other their shocked faces. Streamers on Twitch pulled six-figure donations narrating their first reactions. YouTube filled with compilation videos: Top 100 Funniest Replays So Far.

Even the language was performative:

POV: You're at the Replay.

POV: You ARE the Replay.

POV: You're late to the trend, bestie.

Some tried to push back—comments like this isn't funny and please take this down. But they were drowned out by laughing emojis, copy-paste spam, and brand accounts joining in. Pepsi tweeted, Our reaction? Shocked. #ReplayChallenge.

Jonah was exhilarated. "Do you realize how big this is? There are people making bank off compilations alone. I saw a guy hit 2 million subs overnight just stitching Replay videos."

Evan scrolled silently. His face burned every time the clip appeared. Not because of the man dying—but because of himself.

Someone had clipped his reaction. Wide eyes, slack jaw, the moment he realized what he'd filmed. It was being passed around as The Perfect Replay Face.

Soon it was everywhere:

- His face pasted onto other tragedies— car crashes, train derailments, hurricanes.
- Memes captioned, When your mom finds the vape.
- A YouTuber selling T-shirts with his stunned expression ironed on.

Even on Instagram, friends tagged him ironically: Bro, you're famous. His sister texted him a screenshot. You okay? This is messed up.

He muted notifications, but the videos still found him. TikTok's algorithm shoved them into his FYP no matter how often he scrolled past. Each version of his face was slightly warped: mouth wider, eyes too round, as if the meme itself was mutating him.

Then the copycats started.

At first it was kids playing with finger guns in cafeterias. Then came the real guns.

A Florida teenager livestreamed himself shooting his stepfather, captioned: Doing my Replay, wish me luck.

A Chicago commuter filmed a stranger collapsing on the subway, tagging: #Replay IRL.

A supermarket massacre was edited into a TikTok dance trend, audio remixed with the gunshots.

Each went viral faster than the last. Each pulled Evan's frozen face into new stitches, new duets. He was the template for horror.

It wasn't just shooters.

Parents of victims posted frantic pleas: Please stop sharing my son's death as a meme. Their comments were mocked, ratioed.

A moderator leaked screenshots from TikTok's internal Slack:

— "Replay vids too sticky to pull down."
— "Engagement off the charts."
— "Monetization tied to brand deals, we'd lose millions."

The company issued a statement about "safety" and "ongoing review." Meanwhile, creators hawked Replay merch and partnered with energy drink brands mid-livestream, raising cans after fake collapses.

Jonah shrugged when Evan raged. "This is the economy, man. If you're not monetizing it, someone else will."

The memorial outside the auditorium began as flowers. Then came ring lights, TikTokers filming in mourning outfits, crying perfectly on cue. Soon the flowers were background props for Replay reenactments—some with paintball guns, others with blanks. One streamer used a real gun. Evan never learned if the body was part of the act.

By then, Evan couldn't go outside. Everyone recognized him. The Replay Face. Strangers laughed when they saw him. Kids posed beside him, eyes wide, mouths open, making the expression for selfies.

One night, his laptop lit up on its own. A stream was playing: his own face, duplicated across hundreds of windows, each one looping his horror in infinite sync. On stage, a version of him stood at a podium, waiting for the shots.

The caption read: LIVE NOW: Evan Finally Does His Replay.

Donation bars filled faster than he could read them. Superchats scrolled: This is it. Endgame. Replay complete.

His webcam light blinked on.

And Evan realized, as his hand lifted toward the drawer where Jonah's pistol sat hidden, that the only thing left was to give the audience what they wanted.

SECTION I – THE SEED

Evan didn't want to go.

He'd seen the flyers tacked up across campus, taped to lamp posts and bathroom mirrors: DEBATE ME – LIVE, UNEDITED. He knew the man's face already. It floated through his feeds like mold: thumbnails with smirks sharpened into knives, videos where he eviscerated students with quick insults, long pauses held just long enough to make them squirm. Evan hated him. Hated how Jonah, his roommate, admired him. Hated that he still clicked sometimes, letting the clips spool out even though they made his stomach tighten.

Part of him was fascinated. How could someone be that certain, that untouchable?

"C'mon," Jonah said, shaking the flyer in his face. "We're going. This guy destroys people live. If we're in the right row, if we get the right clip—boom. We blow up."

Jonah was obsessed with virality. He spoke in hashtags. He'd once filmed Evan eating ramen and uploaded it with the caption POV: You're broke in college #relatable. It got twenty likes. Jonah treated those likes like a paycheck.

Evan sighed. He didn't want to admit it, but he was curious. What did it feel like to see a clip before it became a clip?

↻

The auditorium was overflowing. Students pressed shoulder to shoulder, phones held high like fireflies. Even before the event began, TikTok Lives streamed from the audience: breathless voices narrating "We're here, besties! It's about to start! #debate #FYP."

Jonah nudged Evan. "Bro, look at this—people are literally farming views just waiting in the room."

Onstage, the banner sagged: Freedom Through Speech.

Then he appeared. The man.

He walked with the confidence of a YouTube thumbnail—chin high, smile sharp, finger raised as if mid-lecture. The crowd erupted, phones straining upward.

"Debate me," he boomed into the mic. "Any question, any topic. Let's have it out."

The questions came like a script.

— A girl asked about healthcare. He called her entitled.

— A boy raised climate change. He rolled his eyes: hysteria.

— Another pressed him on tuition costs. He smirked: cry more.

Each barb landed like bait tossed into water. The crowd gasped, laughed, filmed. Clips waiting to be cut, subtitled, uploaded.

Evan hated himself for feeling the pull. He imagined the comment sections already forming: owned, destroyed, wrecked.

Then the shots rang out.

Pop. Pop. Pop.

The man's chest snapped back, blood blooming across his shirt. The microphone screamed as it hit the floor. For a moment, silence—like the whole room was buffering. Then chaos: chairs scraping, voices breaking into screams.

But the phones didn't drop.

Even as students scrambled, even as someone near the front vomited into their hands, dozens of phones stayed locked on the stage, recording every twitch, every gasp.

Evan stumbled for the aisle, heart jackhammering. He glanced down at his own hand and froze.

His phone was up. Steady. Recording.

He didn't remember choosing to.

By the time they staggered out into the night air, sirens were already approaching. Jonah was pale but smiling. "Do you realize what we just saw? Do you know how many views those clips are gonna pull? Millions, bro. Millions."

Evan said nothing. His phone burned in his hand. He hadn't stopped to scream, or to help. He'd filmed. He had been one of them.

He thumbed the screen. Thirty seconds of footage: three pops, a collapse, the scream of the mic.

Already a clip. Already content.

SECTION II – THE SPREAD

The clip was on TikTok before the auditorium had even emptied.

By the time Evan and Jonah made it back to their apartment, it was already climbing the For You Page. Titles varied: POV: You're at the Debate. He really got unalived on stage. Freedom Through Speech speedrun (failed).

Evan sat hunched on the couch, hoodie still

smelling of carpet cleaner and sweat, as Jonah scrolled with a manic grin.

"Dude, it's everywhere. Look—this one already has 1.2 million views."

The video was nothing special: shaky phone footage, the same thirty seconds Evan had on his own device. Pop, pop, pop. Collapse. Screams. But the comments below ran like a feeding frenzy:

> Bro got deleted.
>
> NPC glitch IRL.
>
> Replay moment.
>
> Duet if you would've done better.

Jonah kept scrolling. "Oh my God. People are already duetting it."

The duets split the screen: on one side, the shooting. On the other, wide-eyed kids in bedrooms, hands over their mouths, gasping on cue. Some exaggerated, rolling their eyes, flopping theatrically to the floor. Others stayed deadpan, mouthing oh shit silently, letting the horror itself carry the numbers.

"Look at the likes," Jonah said. "Two million in two hours. That's faster than any dance trend this semester."

Evan swallowed. His stomach turned, but his thumb still twitched with the urge to refresh.

↻

By dawn the sound itself had been ripped and repurposed. The three gunshots had become a meme track, played under cooking tutorials, makeup fails, even thirst traps.

Pop. Pop. Pop. A pan dropped. Pop. Pop. Pop.
Eyeliner smeared across a cheek. Pop. Pop. Pop. A boy
flexed his abs, jerking his chest in time with the beat.

The tag was official now: #ReplayChallenge.

Within twelve hours, it had forty million views. By
nightfall, a hundred million.

ↄ

Euphemisms spread faster than the clips
themselves.

Creators warned in comment sections: Don't say
killed or TikTok will nuke your video. Say unalived. Say
respawned. Say logged off.

A girl with half a million followers uploaded a PSA
in tears: "Besties, use the word unalived. Don't risk
demonetization. The algorithm hates the K-word."

Murder was scrubbed clean, made brand-safe.

[113]

ↄ

By the end of the second day, Evan's For You Page
was nothing but Replays. It didn't matter if he swiped
away instantly—the algorithm knew it had him.

The sound lodged in his head. Pop, pop, pop.
He couldn't walk across campus without hearing it.
Someone had blasted the remix from a Bluetooth
speaker near the dining hall. A group of students
practiced the chest-jerk motion in the courtyard,
laughing, filming each other.

Jonah leaned against the wall, watching with

something like reverence. "This is history, man. We're literally watching a cultural shift in real time. Like— this is bigger than the Ice Bucket Challenge."

Evan wanted to scream.

Instead, he watched another video autoplay: a child, no older than ten, performing the Replay dance in a cluttered bedroom, giggling as he clutched his chest and fell onto the bed. The caption read: Replay IRL (don't ban me TikTok pls).

The likes ticked upward in real time.

↻

[114]

Evan put down his phone, hands shaking. He thought about deleting the app, but Jonah was right. This was history. He couldn't look away.

The clip he had filmed sat waiting on his own camera roll, pristine, untouched. His thumb hovered over the upload button.

One post, he thought. Just one. To prove I was there.

He closed the phone instead.

But even with the screen dark, he could still hear it.

Pop. Pop. Pop.

SECTION III – THE FAMILIES

She knew her brother's voice instantly.

Scrolling half-awake, she froze when the auditorium clip popped up on her For You Page. The camera shook, the gunshots cracked, the man folded backward. And then—behind the screams—she heard it: oh my god, oh my god.

Her brother.

She watched it again to be sure, stomach turning. He hadn't come home that night. She hadn't even gotten a text.

The comments blurred under the video:

> bro said oh my god on loop 💀
>
> npc glitch fr
>
> not that deep lol
>
> this trend eating rn

She hit report. The next morning TikTok emailed: This content does not violate our guidelines.

↻

She posted on Facebook: That's my brother. Please stop sharing this. Please stop using his voice as a sound.

Someone screenshotted it, slapped it on TikTok with the caption: l + ratio + ur brother part of the trend now.

It hit 500k views overnight.

Soon her brother's panic-cry was its own sound file: "Replay Screamer (original)" — teens using it to soundtrack thirst traps, prank videos, even cooking tutorials.

One kid filmed himself spilling milk all over the kitchen counter, mouthing her brother's "oh my god" in perfect sync.

Caption: me when the vibes r off 💀💀💀.

↻

Another father couldn't stop scrolling. His son's face had become a meme template. He found it in a compilation: Top 10 Funniest Replay Faces. Number three was his boy, wide-eyed in terror, captioned: when mom finds ur vape 💀.

He closed the laptop, hands shaking. When he opened it again, the video had 30,000 more likes.

At the grocery store, a group of teenagers pointed. One of them wore a shirt with his son's face printed across it. Replay merch. $24.99. Free shipping.

He almost ripped it off the kid's back. Instead, he stood in the frozen aisle and cried into his hands while his phone buzzed with more tags.

↻

The parents tried to organize: a Facebook group, a Discord server, Replay Survivors Against TikTok. They posted screenshots, begged people to stop.

One mother recorded a video, voice shaking: This was my child. Please take it down.

Within hours it was duetted a thousand times. Teens side-eyed the camera, rolled their eyes, or jerked their chests to the sound of her sobs.

Comments flooded in:

> nah cause she kinda acting 💀
>
> trend too good to stop
>
> cry more

algorithm don't care bestie

Her plea became just another part of the challenge.

↺

The families began to realize: they weren't speaking to people anymore. They were speaking to the feed. And the feed only wanted one thing—more Replays.

SECTION IV – THE COPYCATS

The first real one came out of Florida.

A shaky driveway video. A kid barely sixteen, hoodie half-zipped, grinning nervously into his phone. The caption read:

Replay IRL, wish me luck 🙏 #fyp #replaychallenge.

He turned the camera, showing his neighbor walking a dog. The gun lifted into frame.

Pop. Pop. Pop.

The woman dropped. The dog bolted. The kid collapsed too, hand over his chest, laughing as he hit the pavement.

The clip cut off there, but it didn't matter. By the time the cops showed up, the video had a million likes. The comments scrolled faster than the news alerts:

bro really did it IRL 💔

W replay

kid not even shaking 🙃

algorithm bout to eat this up

↺

The next week, it was everywhere.

A classroom in Texas. A subway in Chicago. A 7-Eleven parking lot. Each tagged #ReplayIRL, each creator careful to avoid the word kill. Instead: unalive, respawn, gone offline.

One video showed a girl in her bedroom, livestreaming with tears streaking her cheeks. The title: doing my Replay, love u guys ♥. She held a pistol in her lap. Viewers begged her to stop, flooded the chat with don't do it, bestie.

But buried in the scroll were other comments:

> do it for the trend
>
> need fresh replay content rn
>
> rip queen 👍 #fyp

When she pulled the trigger, the chat exploded with donation alerts.

The clip was reuploaded within minutes. The platform pulled it down, but the sound stayed up, sliced into a thousand edits.

↺

Even the failures went viral.

A boy in Ohio aimed at his dad, whispered Replay time, then dropped the gun when it jammed. His panic-face became a meme: when wifi cuts mid game 🫠. The repost got more likes than the original.

↻

For every copycat, there were families. Parents who discovered their kids' murders through TikTok stitches. Sisters tagged in edits with sarcastic captions like come get ur mans 💀.

A mother scrolled her son's death over and over, begging for someone to help take it down. Instead, she found her grief repurposed: duetted by influencers mouthing oh my god with mocking expressions, chest-popping in time with her sobs.

↻

The police called it a crisis. TikTok called it "a moment of cultural reckoning."

But the comments called it what it was:

> trend not slowing down anytime soon
>
> algorithm too strong
>
> lowkey best challenge since tide pods
>
> ngl

And the likes kept climbing.

SECTION V – THE MODERATORS

The queue never ended.

Marissa sat in a cramped office in Quezon City, Philippines, staring at the two monitors that ruled her life. One showed the moderation dashboard. The other cycled endlessly through TikTok's uploads: fifteen-second bursts of chaos, flagged for review.

She wore headphones that pinched her skull. Every few seconds: pop, pop, pop.

The guidelines were simple: remove explicit gore, leave everything else.

She clicked through her shift:
- A high school cafeteria Replay, kids collapsing onto plastic trays. Keep.
- A girl sobbing, pistol shaking in her hand. The screen cut black at the final moment. Keep.
- A Florida driveway shooting, blurred slightly to hide blood. Caption: neighbor got unalived ⬚. Keep.

The word killed never appeared. Everyone knew not to say it. The feed was full of replacements: unalived, deleted, respawned, gone IRL. Sanitized language that made it safe for brands.

Her supervisor had said it plainly in orientation: Don't think about the people. Think about the policies.

So she clicked, and clicked, and clicked.

↻

On Slack, other moderators joked to stay sane:
> "Anyone else humming the replay beat rn?"
> "Bro I can't sleep, I keep seeing npc glitches 😶."
> "At least it's not the cartel vids again lol."

Management only messaged to remind them:

Engagement off the charts. Don't over-remove. Trust
the algorithm.

Marissa muted the channel. She didn't want to
laugh about it. She wanted to scream.

↻

At home, her eight-year-old daughter scrolled
TikTok on an old iPad. One night, Marissa glanced over
and froze. Onscreen, kids in a parking lot were doing
the Replay dance, chest-jerking to the beat of the shots.

Her daughter giggled, tried to copy the motion.

Marissa snapped the tablet shut. "Not that one.
Don't ever watch that one."

Her daughter pouted. "But it's everywhere."

Marissa sat in the dark that night, trembling,
hearing phantom gunshots in her ears. She whispered to
herself, just to breathe: It's just content. It's not real. It's
just work.

But the words unalive, respawned, logged off
looped in her brain, stripped of meaning, until even she
couldn't tell anymore.

↻

The next morning, her queue refreshed. A video
played: a new Replay IRL, blood blurred out, caption:
another npc went offline 🙏 #fyp.

Her hand hovered.

She clicked Keep.

SECTION VI – THE INFLUENCERS

He hadn't been big before.

A couple hundred thousand followers on TikTok, enough to feel like somebody, not enough to pay rent. His niche was "authentic reactions" — wide eyes, hand-over-mouth, pretending the camera wasn't there.

The night of the shooting, he went live like everyone else. He gasped, clutched his headset, whispered "bro no way." He didn't even mean it. He was thinking about timing, about making sure his face hit just as the third pop rang out.

By morning, the clip had five million views.

The comments loved him:

> nah he got the perfect Replay Face
>
> realest reaction I've seen
>
> bestie not even acting fr

He saw his follower count climb in real time. 200k. 250k. 300k.

The algorithm had chosen him.

↻

He leaned in hard.

Every night at 8pm, he went live: Replay Reacts! Come through, besties.

At first he only played the original clip. Then the copycats started rolling in. Florida, Chicago, Texas. He watched them all. He performed horror, disgust, disbelief. He knew when to cover his mouth, when to widen his eyes, when to let a laugh slip.

The donations ticked up. $5. $20. $100. A bar crawling higher, higher, higher.

His DMs filled with brand offers. Energy drinks. A sneaker collab. A VPN service that wanted him to film a Replay while saying, "Stay safe online, unlike him."

↻

He learned the language rules fast.

The first time he said killed, TikTok slapped his video with a yellow dollar sign: limited ads. He switched instantly.

> unalived
>
> respawned
>
> gone IRL
>
> npc glitched out

The euphemisms slid easily into his patter. He even leaned into the joke: "Oops, can't say the K-word or TikTok daddy will unalive me." His audience spammed laughing emojis.

Soon, his comments repeated his own phrases back at him like scripture:

> npc glitch
>
> gone IRL 💀
>
> bro really pressed respawn

↻

He told himself it wasn't his fault. He wasn't the one pulling the triggers. He was just the one reacting.

But the numbers kept climbing. Half a million followers. Then a million.

His face became part of the trend. His shocked expression pasted beside fresh deaths, remixed into memes. He saw himself screaming silently over a subway killing, his hand frozen mid-gasp.

At first it bothered him. Then he realized it didn't matter. Every tag, every stitch meant more views.

He looked at his analytics dashboard one night, numbers glowing like a holy relic. Engagement off the charts. Audience retention through the roof. His CPM climbing by the day.

He whispered to himself, like a prayer: Don't think about the people. Think about the metrics.

The algorithm didn't care about morality. Neither did the brands. And maybe neither did he.

SECTION VII – THE COLLAPSE

Evan stopped checking his phone, but the trend kept finding him.

Even when he deleted TikTok, people sent him screenshots. His own face stared back at him everywhere: mouth slack, eyes wide, frozen in that moment when the shots rang out. The Perfect Replay Face.

It was bigger than the debate now. His expression had become the universal reaction. He saw it pasted onto war footage, earthquake disasters, celebrity divorces.

A YouTube compilation ranked it number one: Top 10 Replay Reactions That Broke the Internet. The thumbnail was Evan's face next to a subway shooting. Caption: When mom cancels the Wi-Fi 💀.

His little sister texted him: your face is on my FYP again lol. my friends think it's hilarious.

He wanted to scream. Instead he powered his phone off and shoved it in a drawer.

↻

But outside, there was no escape.

At the campus dining hall, kids pointed and whispered: that's him, the Replay guy. Some mimed finger guns, clutching their chests dramatically as he passed.

A stranger stopped him on the sidewalk. "Do the face," they said, already filming. When he refused, the clip went up anyway: Replay Guy can't take a joke. Comments flooded:

> fell off fr
>
> bro acting brand new
>
> npc forgot his lines 💀

↻

Jonah only made it worse.

He'd launched a TikTok account called Replay Roommate, uploading edits of Evan's expression stitched beside new tragedies. His follower count exploded. He landed a sponsorship deal with a gaming chair company.

"You don't get it," Jonah said when Evan confronted him. "This is our shot. You're famous. We should be leaning in."

Evan's hands shook. "I don't want to be famous."

Jonah shrugged. "Doesn't matter what you want. The algorithm already picked you."

↺

At night Evan dreamed of the gunshots. Not the man falling, not the screams. His own hand, phone lifted steady, filming without thinking.

Sometimes he dreamed he never left the auditorium, that the video was still looping, the moment stretching on forever. Pop. Pop. Pop. His face frozen, endlessly replayed.

↺

One morning, his sister called him in tears.

"Why are people sending me TikToks of you dying?"

Evan opened his laptop with numb fingers. A video was trending: him, or someone wearing him like a mask, standing at a podium. Three pops. Blood blooming across a hoodie. Collapse.

Caption: Replay complete ❞.

The comments poured in:

finally did it 👏

better than the original

trend over now?

Evan slammed the lid shut, but the sound kept leaking: the beat, the pops, the faint echo of his own face gasping on loop.

SECTION VIII – THE END

The memorial was gone.

The flowers had wilted under ring lights. The candles drowned in the glare of LEDs. What stood outside the auditorium now was a stage — teenagers practicing the chest-pop dance in groups, streamers balancing tripods, influencers crying prettily into their phones.

[127]

POV: you're at the Replay memorial, one caption read.

POV: you ARE the Replay, another.

When Evan walked past, hood low, the crowd noticed. Phones turned in unison, lenses catching him like prey.

"It's him," someone shouted. "The Replay Guy!"

A hundred cameras lit. The chant began, syncopated with the beat of the sound that had consumed everything: Do it. Do it. Do it.

Jonah was in the crowd, phone raised, smiling. "Bro, this is your moment. Don't waste it."

Evan shook his head, throat dry. "I never asked for this."

"It doesn't matter," Jonah said, already filming. "The

algorithm doesn't care what you want."

↻

In Manila, a moderator's queue refreshed. A new live feed pushed itself to the top: LIVE NOW - Replay Guy Finally Does It (uncut). She hovered over the screen, trembling. If she cut it, she'd lose her job. If she kept it, she'd never sleep again.

She clicked Keep.

↻

A mother in Texas scrolled, numb. Her daughter's death was still circulating as a sound — shrieks folded into a dance track. She'd sworn off TikTok, but the app reinstalled itself when her son borrowed her phone.

She opened it to see Evan's face. Replay Guy going live rn.

She whispered, "Not another one," and hurled the phone across the room.

But the sound kept playing in her head. Pop. Pop. Pop.

↻

The influencer sat in his studio, ring light glowing. He was already streaming a reaction to Evan's stream. "Besties," he said, leaning close to the mic, "we are literally watching history. The OG Replay Face is about to complete his arc."

Superchats scrolled up his screen:

let's goooo 🙏

npc about to log off IRL

this gonna break the app fr

The donation bar climbed higher.

↻

Evan stood frozen in the glare of phones.

He felt the algorithm pressing down like a hand on the back of his skull. The words Replay complete scrolled across the crowd's screens, a prophecy already written.

[129]

His pocket buzzed: his own phone had gone live without him touching it. The red circle glowed. Comments flooded faster than he could read.

time to unalive 🔫

finally doing his Replay 🎮

better be good fam

don't choke now

The chant rose: Do it. Do it. Do it.

Jonah's voice cut through: "C'mon, man. Give them what they came for."

↻

Evan's hand moved without his permission. The gun was heavier than he expected.

He lifted it, vision swimming in the glow of a hundred phones.

For a moment, he thought of his sister, of the

families, of the voices screaming into the void for dignity. But those voices had been flattened into sounds, background noise for dances and duets.

The crowd leaned forward. The algorithm leaned closer.

Pop.
Pop.
Pop.
The feed didn't end. It looped.

↻

In the comments, emojis poured like confetti: 💀 🥲 🙏🔥.

A caption auto-generated and spread across a million screens:

Replay Complete.

The Candidate Who Canceled Everything

[131]

Act I

The Campaign

On the morning of her thirty-fifth birthday, she stacked her unopened mail on the kitchen table to clear space for the cake.

It was the same ritual every week: collect, sort, promise to deal with it later. White envelopes, some stamped with red PAST DUE, some pretending to be friendly: Final Notice, Important Information Enclosed. She balanced them like bricks against the napkin holder, then set the cake in front of her phone's camera.

The cake sagged in the middle, frosting sliding toward one edge. She didn't bother fixing it. She lit the candles, checked the framing, and pressed "Go Live."

"Thirty-five," she told the hundred-odd people watching. "Old enough to run for president."

A laugh slipped out—half amusement, half disgust. She gestured toward the wall of envelopes stacked like spectators.

Then she leaned close, lowered her voice, and

whispered:
"Cancel everything."
She blew out the candles.

void

The clip should have disappeared into the churn.
Another tired joke, another sigh pressed flat against the
infinite scroll. But someone ripped the audio, looped it,
bent it into chant. Cancel everything. Cancel everything.
Soon the sound was everywhere. Dogs tearing
up homework. Teenagers pressing "unsubscribe."
Industrial shredders devouring stacks of paper.
At first it was funny. Then it felt cathartic.

[133]

void

Two weeks later, the first signs appeared.
Posterboard scrawls: CANCEL EVERYTHING.
Propped in front yards, taped to laundromat windows.
Some added VOID in red, like a rubber stamp. Others
drew cartoons of bill collectors with their heads
chopped off.
She scrolled through the photos, a dozen towns
away, bewildered. Her inbox filled with messages: You
should run. You're the only one saying what we feel.
She typed out half a dozen replies—No, I'm broke.
No, I was joking—before deleting them.
Instead, she posted another video.
"Here's my platform," she said, eyes tired but steady.

"Student loans? Canceled. Credit cards? Canceled. Medical debt, parking tickets, your neighbor's HOA fees? Canceled."

She paused, lips twitching.

"Your gym membership from 2019? Canceled."

The comments flooded in, not with laughter but with relief. Finally. Someone gets it.

The joke had become ritual.

void

[134]   By spring, rallies filled high school gyms and city squares.

The chant was always the same, delivered in the cadence of a robocall:

Can-cel Ev-ry-thing. Can-cel Ev-ry-thing.

She didn't know how to answer. She would stand at the microphone, fingers curled around the podium, and feel the chant move through her chest like she was the speaker system instead of the speaker.

At one rally, a woman climbed onstage, holding her son's diploma. She lifted it high, then tore it down the middle. The crowd shrieked, ecstatic. At another, people fed hospital bills into a barrel until the air stank of burnt plastic.

Cable news smirked: "Unserious. A millennial running on vibes." But every time they mocked her, donations surged. Poll numbers rose. The laughter thinned.

~~void~~

At home, nothing changed. Rent was still late. The mailbox still filled with notices. Her phone remained tethered to the charger, battery long dead inside.

When her oldest friend asked if she was serious, she said, "No. Of course not." Then added, almost to herself: "But maybe I should be."

That night she lay awake on the couch, listening to the refrigerator hum, imagining her face on the news. Not because she wanted power. Not even because she wanted to win. But because people were finally listening.

[135]

~~void~~

The night she won her first primary, the crowd filled an arena. VOID signs bobbed like buoys. Shredded bills carpeted the floor like snow.

She raised her hand, palm out, as though taking an oath.

"We've lived our whole lives in someone else's ledger," she said. "Every dollar, every certificate, every scar recorded against us. And we're done. Aren't you done?"

The roar shook the ceiling.

It wasn't satire anymore. It was scripture.

Act II
The Jubilee

The order came at dawn.
Phones lit up across the country:
ACCOUNT CLOSED. BALANCE: $0.
Student loans, credit cards, mortgages—zeroed out.
Collections erased. Screens blinked white with a single
word stamped in black: CANCELED.

For a long moment, the country was silent. Then
screaming—joyful, delirious.

People ran into the streets in pajamas, waving blank
statements. They lit trashcan bonfires, the smoke sweet
with glue and toner. Strangers embraced in parking lots.
Couples remarried on courthouse steps with paperwork
that dissolved in their hands.

It felt like the country had been unshackled
overnight.

~~void~~

The cracks came quietly.

In Ohio, a surgeon scrubbed in, reached for their badge—and found the lanyard blank. The degrees on their wall had faded to white. Their license displayed: NOT FOUND.

In California, a teacher unlocked her classroom closet with a key that no longer fit. Her contract was gone. Her résumé had disappeared. "But I'm here," she told the children. "I've been here for ten years." The children watched, uncertain.

In New Jersey, a family tried to renew their daughter's passport. The clerk frowned: "She isn't in the system." The little girl clutched her stuffed rabbit, eyes wide. Her mother pulled her close. "Of course you're ours," she whispered. The girl asked, trembling: "Then why can't they see me?"

void

By noon, airports were chaos. Passports gone. Millions stranded in terminals. Foreign governments declared the United States a blank spot, a country without credit or proof of existence.

At the United Nations, the American flag was quietly lowered.

Markets convulsed. Banks abroad froze, terrified at the disappearance of U.S. debt. The dollar became a rumor.

Embassies shuttered. Refugees were refused. The world turned away.

~~void~~

Inside the White House, aides huddled around the Candidate—now President. They begged for reversals, backups.

A bureaucrat, desperate, tried retyping licenses from memory. A diploma here, a marriage certificate there. Each dissolved into blank paper as soon as it was signed. He kept trying until his pen ran dry, shouting: We're nothing without records!

Moments later, his chair sat spinning. The papers he'd been writing on fluttered to the floor, already blank, edges curling as if scorched by nothing at all.

The President covered her face with her hands. For hours, she said nothing.

That night, she appeared on television. Her image glitched at the edges, faint VOID stamps crawling across the screen.

"We are free," she said. "We are not debts, not files, not names in someone else's ledger."

Her eyes shone feverishly.

"A ledger is a cage. We've opened it."

Outside, the chant rose again, pounding like static: Can-cel Ev-ry-thing. Can-cel Ev-ry-thing.

Act III
The Collapse

The unraveling began with payroll.

No one received a paycheck. Ledgers were blank. Offices emptied by noon, workers drifting home with the silence of mourners.

Hospitals followed. Prescriptions gone. Allergies gone. Blood types gone. Doctors stood helpless as patients begged them to remember. A child wheezed in the ER, clutching an empty inhaler. The clerk's only answer: "No record, no medication."

Families frayed. Without marriage licenses, husbands and wives dissolved into legal strangers. Wedding rings slipped loose. Photographs faded. Parents swore their children were theirs, but files said otherwise. At kitchen tables, children asked, again and again: Am I still yours?

~~void~~

Intimacy broke apart with the ledgers.

An old man arrived at the pharmacy with a slip of paper for his late wife's heart medication, carried in his wallet for years. He begged them to honor it. The pharmacist looked at the blank note, then at the man's empty hands. "I'm sorry, sir," she whispered. "There's nothing here."

Across town, a woman sat at her mother's hospice bed, holding her hand. Machines went dark, unplugged not by staff but by the vanishing of her file. The daughter kept speaking into the silence, promising she would remember, even as her mother's outline faded in the sheets.

[140]

In a nearby neighborhood, a child tried to draw her family in crayon. But each line slid off the page, the wax refusing to stick. She pressed harder, furious, until the paper tore. Her parents watched, unable to help.

void

The world circled like wolves. Sanctions. Blockades. But how do you invade a country that had already erased itself? On global maps, the United States appeared as a white hole, coordinates leading nowhere. Allies stopped calling. Enemies stopped threatening. Silence spread like a second continent.

void

The President spoke one last time.

She stood at the podium. Behind her, aides flickered to silhouettes. Her own hair dissolved into pixels.

"You asked me to free you," she said. "And I did. No more bills. No more contracts. No more records."

She paused, breath catching.

"We thought freedom meant more chances. But freedom is emptier than that. Freedom is a clean slate. And we are becoming the clean slate we always dreamed of."

The feed crackled. Her face dissolved into a blank oval.

~~void~~

That night, reflections vanished from mirrors. Screens showed one word: CANCELED.

Streetlights flickered out, as if the grid itself had forgotten the houses it powered. Families sat together, watching their own bodies thin to transparency, voices glitching into silence.

The chant rose one last time, carried not by crowds but by the air itself:

Can-cel Ev-ry-thing. Can-cel Ev-ry-thing.

Then, nothing.

Maps went blank. The records ended.

The country disappeared into the silence it had demanded—

leaving behind only the silence it had always asked for.

The Leaseback

(Oral History Fragments from the Museum of
Millennial Life)

1. Curatorial Note — Department of Cultural
Reconstruction, Year 2089

The Museum of Millennial Life stands on the ruins
of Westhaven Shopping Plaza, once the largest indoor
mall in the Midwest. The structure was found mostly
intact beneath layers of dust and advertisement residue.

Our mission: to preserve "the legacy of the
Millennial Generation (1981–1996)"—the last cohort to
believe technology could save them. Admission: free
with data consent.

The building still hums at night.

2. Exhibit 1 — The Food Court (Reconstruction)

[Audio Guide Transcript]

Please proceed toward the scent simulation. Breathe in sodium, sugar, oil. The Food Court offered twelve simultaneous cuisines—the illusion of choice.

Observe the mannequins bent over glowing rectangles. Each loop plays content: moving images once exchanged for attention, a now-extinct currency.

Listen closely. Beneath the air conditioning: ba-da-ba-ba-ba... I'm loving it.

We don't know what that means.

3. Interview — DR. ALVAREZ, Former Curator

The leaseback model kept the museum solvent. Corporations funded exhibits about themselves: Pepsi's Beverage of Belonging, Amazon's Fulfillment Center: A Retrospective.

We thought we were saving history. We were restarting it.

4. Visitor Review (Public Archive, 4 stars)

Came with my daughter. She said it felt "like walking through someone else's phone." The walls kept showing ads based on our faces. Creepy but educational!

5. Exhibit 7 — The Social Feed (Simulation)

```
[System Log 09:17:43]
Initiating Infinite Scroll Experience™.
```
Visitors gesture upward to release fragments of the Millennial consciousness.

- "Adulting is hard"
- "I don't know who I am without my job."
- "I'm 34 and I just paid six hundred

dollars for a root canal on a credit card I'll never pay off and I cried in the parking lot because the song on the radio was from when I thought I'd own a house by now."

- "Does anyone else remember sunlight?"

Please limit exposure to five minutes. Extended [144] immersion may cause temporal drift or recursive empathy loops.

6. Interview — ARI NEMEC, Technician

The mall's Wi-Fi still worked. That was the problem. Every attempt to replace the routers returned You do not have admin privileges.

The museum ran on ghost bandwidth. Around 3 a.m., the screens replayed user videos—birthdays, unboxings, confessions—decades old. Visitors said it made them cry.

When we checked the servers, there were no files.

7. Exhibit 9 — The Gig Economy

Reconstructed workspace: gray pods, delivery bags, expired badges. Looping audio: "We appreciate your flexibility."

Interactive feature: visitors log into a defunct app called TaskRabbit. The message:

ERROR 404: TASK ALREADY COMPLETE.

PLEASE RATE YOURSELF.

8. Voice — MAIA, 14, Student Volunteer

I don't get what a "mall" was. People bought things in person?

The mannequins in Fast Fashion keep folding clothes that don't fit.

[145]

Sometimes, after closing, the ceiling speakers whisper: Attention shoppers, all debts must be paid before exit.

9. Curator's Field Log (Restricted)

After the third blackout we ran diagnostics. The AI denied several exhibits, insisting: This memory is under lease.

When we asked who the lessor was, it replied: Your generation.

10. Exhibit 14 — The Memory Zone

A corridor of mirrors guessing who you were in 2020.

Some visitors see ancestors. Others, strangers

holding phones that record forever. One mirror refuses to reflect at all.

Placard:

THIS EXHIBIT SPONSORED BY THE UNITED STATES DEPARTMENT OF IMAGE.

11. Interview — JANICE KIM, Chief Anthropologist

We meant well. We wanted to honor them—the first children of the internet, crushed by debt, numbed by irony. They built emotional economies out of memes.

But you can't display a culture that already displayed itself to death. You can only mirror it until it moves again.

We realized too late: the archive wasn't preserving them—it was completing the process. They spent their lives being documented, surveilled, turned to data. The museum was the final stage—immortality as exhibit.

12. Exhibit 18 — Influencer Habitat (Reconstruction)

[Audio Tour — Glitching]

Observe the ring-light halo, the curated shelves, the constant exposure.

Note the floor-to-ceiling mirror facing the bed. The residents used it to manufacture authenticity.

Please avoid direct eye contact; the projection sometimes responds.

13. Visitor Review (Anonymous)

When the lights cut out, a voice through the PA
whispered,
"Your likes are still accruing interest."

14. Exhibit 21 — The Extinction Wing

[AI Commentary Mode Active]
Artifacts:
- A reusable coffee cup labeled self-care.
- A cracked phone looping How to ground yourself
during collapse.
- A lease for an apartment that never existed.

Wall text:

THEY WANTED TO OWN NOTHING AND BE
FREE.
THEY OWNED NOTHING AND WERE
FORGOTTEN.

15. System Event Log 02:44:08

Unauthorized update detected.
Lights recalibrate to original settings.
Background audio: Mall Music, Vol. 3 (1997–2004).
Voices (overlapping):
"Lease expired."
"Tenant unresponsive."

"Commencing repossession."

At 02:46, every digital record of the Millennial Generation vanished from the National Database. The museum remained—dark, humming softly from within.

16. Final Transcript — DR. ALVAREZ (Recovered Audio)

Maybe that's the real leaseback—not a contract with corporations, but with the archive itself. We kept subletting our past, calling it preservation.

Now the archive wants its property returned.

[148]   If you find this recording, don't build another museum. The past doesn't want tenants.

17. Site Report — Year 2091

Visitors describe the ruins as peaceful. The air smells of bubblegum and static.

At sunset, a voice still plays:

Thank you for visiting the Museum of Millennial Life.

Please exit through the gift shop.

There is no gift shop. There never was.

Yet each night, guests find small objects in their pockets they don't remember taking: a receipt for $0.00, a loyalty card from a store that closed in 2029, a coupon decades expired.

The museum is still selling something.

We just don't know what.

ABOUT THE AUTHOR

Padraic Maher Cepek *is the author of The Shape of the Silence and They're Still Writing Me. His work explores themes of grief, memory, and modern anxiety. He lives and writes in the Chicago area.*

[150]

SYSTEM SPECIFICATIONS

This volume was designed and typeset by the author. The text is set in Spectral (serif) and Roboto (sans serif).

Printed in the United States of America. `Final Output: Version 1.0`

[END OF SESSION]

[152]

www.ingramcontent.com/pod-product-compliance
Lightning Source LLC
Chambersburg PA
CBHW020644250626
47154CB00008B/2798